# FIRST LOVE

A SINGLE DAD NEXT DOOR ROMANCE

CELESTE FALL

HOT AND STEAMY ROMANCE

# CONTENTS

| | |
|---|---|
| *Blurb* | vii |
| 1. Chapter One | 1 |
| 2. Chapter Two | 5 |
| 3. Chapter Three | 8 |
| 4. Chapter Four | 10 |
| 5. Chapter Five | 14 |
| 6. Chapter Six | 18 |
| 7. Chapter Seven | 21 |
| 8. Chapter Eight | 25 |
| 9. Chapter Nine | 28 |
| 10. Chapter Ten | 31 |
| 11. Chapter Eleven | 34 |
| 12. Chapter Twelve | 37 |
| 13. Chapter Thirteen | 43 |
| 14. Chapter Fourteen | 49 |
| 15. Chapter Fifteen | 56 |
| 16. Chapter Sixteen | 58 |
| 17. Chapter Seventeen | 63 |
| 18. Chapter Eighteen | 67 |
| 19. Chapter Nineteen | 73 |
| Sign Up to Receive Free Books | 77 |
| Preview of A Billionaire's Treasure | 78 |
| A Billionaire's Treasure | 81 |
| Lola | 83 |
| Arsen | 88 |
| Lola | 92 |
| Arsen | 99 |
| Lola | 105 |
| A Billionaire's Possession | 113 |
| Lola | 115 |

| | |
|---|---|
| Arsen | 123 |
| *Other Books By This Author* | 127 |
| *Copyright* | 129 |

Made in "The United States" by:

Celeste Fall

© Copyright 2020 –Celeste Fall

ISBN: 978-1-64808-059-3

**ALL RIGHTS RESERVED.** No part of this publication may be reproduced or transmitted in any form whatsoever, electronic, or mechanical, including photocopying, recording, or by any informational storage or retrieval system without express written, dated and signed permission from the author

 Created with Vellum

# BLURB

*Thirty-four-year-old Clay Booth had it all: a satisfying career, tons of money, a son he loved to distraction, and all the female attention he wanted. After a tumultuous marriage ended in Parker's mother's suicide, Clay vowed to have nothing but meaningless sex. However, he had not reckoned on the allure of smart, breathtakingly beautiful Virginia Matthew, the naïve, virginal girl next door. Clay's pursuit of her was complicated by the fact that the owner of his building—Virginia's promiscuous mother—was stalking him. Will his crush on Virginia make him break his promise to have no meaningful relations with women? To what lengths will Clay to make this young virgin happy?*

*"My sister warned me to stay away from the trusting girl next door However, what she didn't factor in to this situation was that I'd fall head over heels in love with this girl. Her hot skin tantalized my sleep. Her moist, luscious lips begged for mine to wed hers when I tried to concentrate at work. I could hear her tinkling laugh in my dreams. How can I get out from under her spell? What am I going to do? There's no happy ending in sight, no matter which path I take."*

*"Wow! This is no boy next door. Clay Booth is all man. Every time he fixes me with those piercing, blue eyes, I go all soft inside. My body yearns for him at night. My dreams are filled with hot, sweaty images of him kissing me all over. I think about him night and day. Those soft, exciting lips beckon me to discover regions I've never dreamed about. I feel like such a naughty girl. What's happening to me? Mother warned me that this would not end well. Alas! For once, mother could be right.*

# 1
## CHAPTER ONE

Deanna Matthews fluffed her artfully-streaked blonde hair and straightened the jacket of her Chanel suit. She smiled at her reflection in the mirror of her penthouse apartment. Taking an atypical moment to self-reflect, Deanna looked around the tastefully-appointed apartment and allowed herself to feel proud of her success. When her marriage had ended in a nasty divorce nearly sixteen years ago, Deanna had swallowed the shame of being the jilted wife and looked for a way to provide a good life for herself and her young daughter, Virginia, then a shy six-year-old.

Walking over to the balcony, Deanna stepped outside and surveyed the stunning view from her home. Even from here, she could see the Matthews and Martin Realty billboards that graced benches, buses, and buildings throughout Panama City Beach. Her photograph on them was ten years old and in need of an update, but nevertheless ...

*I still look good.* Her full lips, still filler-free, curved in another wide, trademark smile, the kind that many looked at and mistakenly judged to be naïvely trusting. Its owner, however, was anything but. Deanna was a survivor. On the heels of her acrimonious divorce, deserted by people she'd once considered friends, she had struck out entirely on her own. Through sweat and tears that her former acquaintances could never have fathomed, she'd formed a real estate partnership and earned the admiration of the business community. Twice voted local realtor of the year, she now owned the Sea Urchin Luxury Condominiums where she lived, amongst many other beachfront high rises.

Walking back inside, her eyes drifted to the mantle with the carefully shined awards she'd accumulated. At the back of the apartment, she heard the TV going, probably left on by a maid. A familiar voice caught Deanna's ear and she grimaced, realizing it was *that* hour. Exactly at this time, every day for over twenty years, her ex, Bernie Matthews, dished out a daily dose of advice to needy housewives. He was Seattle's answer to Dr. Phil and Dr. Fraser Crane all rolled into one. Bernie, a licensed psychologist with only mediocre success in his practice, had carved out a career as a TV psychologist with his self-important, outspoken style. He had a niche market with the over-forties female viewing audience, which Deanna always found ironic as Bernie preferred his women half that age.

Even his voice was greasy. Deanna cringed at the thought that she had ever found him appealing. Bernie hadn't been a good husband. He hadn't even been a good father. He'd always been more concerned about his career than his family.

She walked away from the noise, heading toward the kitchen for the last dregs of her espresso. Instead of the tepid remains she'd expected, she found a fresh demi tasse laid out by one of her staff and made a mental note to remember the thoughtfulness at Christmas. Idly, she sipped the steaming brew and mused over the lack of contact between her only child and her ex.

It was just as well, Deanna thought, tapping perfect nails

against the gleaming, granite counter. Her philandering husband had always had a preference for younger women. If the Seattle social pages were any indication, that hadn't changed. Shy and awkward Virginia didn't need to be dragged into that rat's nest of social flurry. As extroverted as Deanna and Bernie were, it was no wonder Virginia had grown up to become the polar opposite of her gregarious, frequently bitterly at odds, parents.

As a result, probably, of seeing one too many louche soirees, Virginia now had few friends. Those she did have all shared an online interest in marine life—like that nerdy Arty Stone who, Deanna thought, was the epitome of the word *geek*. He and Virginia had never met in person—Deanna wasn't even sure where Arty lived. But, ever since Virginia had discovered a marine-life chatroom, she and Arty had been in daily contact.

Shaking off her momentary mood, Deanna shrugged. Yes, she admittedly had little room to criticize Bernie. Since the divorce, Deanna, tanned, toned, and looking at least a decade younger than her mid-fifties, had developed a taste for nubile, young men. She was discrete about it, but, after all, a girl had needs. Why not scratch that itch with someone attractive, energetic, and eager? Deanna's real estate business brought her in contact with a continuous supply of men with surfer bodies who wanted nothing more than she did: a quick, enthusiastic coupling with no strings attached.

Virginia was routinely horrified by her mother's 'cougar' antics—God, Deanna hated that word—but really, what was the harm? She had just sold the other penthouse to a tall, dark, and handsome, billionaire, Clay Booth. He was a touch more acerbic than most men she had briefly dated, but his looks made up for any lack in social graces. He didn't appear attracted to her yet—yet being the key. She had seldom met a man of any age who could resist her charms, and Deanna Matthews was not one to fold when a challenge arose.

She put her cup in the dishwasher, took the bottle of chilled champagne from its customary bucket, plucked two crystal flutes from the cabinet, and added a crystal dish of caviar and a bowl of chocolate-dipped strawberries from the fridge.

"Buckle up, big boy," she said as she walked out of her apartment and straight across the hall, to where Clay had bought the last unit in her building—at a seven-figure price—without even blinking. Deanna's commission on the sale would be mind boggling and she had every intention of celebrating.

She rang Clay's door bell and struck a seductive pose, murmuring, "Welcome to my world. Let the celebration begin."

## CHAPTER TWO

Clay walked through his brand-new apartment, needing to traverse quite a distance to get to the front door. After seeing it on Skype, his ocean-obsessed son, who was the whole reason he'd bought the place, had joked that they needed to install "one of those walking sidewalk things." Clay hadn't disagreed.

He picked up the pace when the bell rang again, even though he didn't usually hurry for much of anybody—not since he'd earned his first billion. Ever since, the money had continued to roll in, and with it, people's automatic respect, a concept that still sometimes confused him. Walking past a glossy brochure on an equally glossy end table that the decorator had purchased, Clay's eyes moved over the Bay County tourism logo, the group for which he was now working with, marketing 'medical holidays' to northerners who needed age-related surgeries. The idea was they could get treatment in one of the country's fine medical facilities and convalesce in a condo facing the ocean. Clay's job was to work with the stakeholders and sell the idea in cities like Boston, New York, St. Louis, and Chicago.

It had all worked out well, he mused, nearing the door and taking a guess at who was behind the impatient buzzing. The penthouse at Sea Urchin was perfect. There were lots of room. It was private. It had state-of-the-art security. All in all, it was a win for medicine, a win for realty, a win for seniors ...

And a win for him, he congratulated himself as he answered the door and swept his eyes over Deanna Matthews' bombshell body. From the time Clay had strolled into the realty offices of Matthews and Martin, Clay had sensed Deanna was eager to offer more than real estate. *Yes,* he thought, eyeing the champagne and strawberries in her carefully manicured hands. *She is a full-service provider.*

She was just the type of woman Clay favored. Beautiful. No strings. No promises. Just hot, sweaty, loud, monkey sex.

"This is a nice surprise." His eyes swept the voluptuous Deanna from head to toe as he accepted the welcome basket. *Yummy,* he thought. He wasn't looking at the welcome basket.

"I had some last-minute paperwork for you to sign," purred Deanna as she slid by Clay. "So, I thought we'd kill two birds with one stone and toast your new home ...unless you're busy settling in."

"What's to settle in?" asked Clay. "The decorator did his bit. Her bit? I'm going to let Parker help decorate his room so it will feel more like home."

"His bit. When does Parker arrive?" asked Deanna, closing the door firmly behind her without invitation. "I'd love to meet him. Perhaps we can get together for dinner and he can meet my little girl, Virginia."

"Parker is finishing his school year in Houston," Clay explained. "I have him enrolled at Bay Academy for August."

"What's he interested in?" asked Deanna. "My little girl has some interesting hobbies. Is he excited about the move?"

He wondered about how little her daughter could be, when, as well-preserved as she was, Deanna was at least somewhere in the vicinity of 50. "He's not unexcited about it." Clay shrugged. "Parker's kind of moved around a lot because of my job. He's an odd kid with unusual interests. He won't miss Texas because he's not leaving friends. At the moment, he's consumed by facts about dolphins and sharks. Not your typical kid at all, so he has a hard time making friends."

"My daughter is working at Gulf World this summer," Deanna commented. "She's teaching dolphins to do something or other. Maybe they could get together and talk? Perhaps Virginia could even show Parker the dolphins."

"If she'd do that," said Clay. "I'd be forever in your debt."

"Let's crack open this champagne and sample this caviar. We can talk about how you can repay me over breakfast."

"Let me get that champagne popped open," Clay said easily, enjoying the moment, even though he wasn't about to climb bed with his realtor. Not a good business move, however much his lower half disagreed. He'd let her down gently, after they drank enough.

## CHAPTER THREE

Deanna woke up the next morning in her own room, to an empty bed, but it didn't faze her. Much. While she was admittedly disappointed at having been gently but firmly put off by Clay the night before, the evening had, nevertheless, been an enjoyable one. Clay was nearly as good a conversationalist as Deanna imagined he would've been in bed. Not that she'd completely given up that hope; that wasn't how she'd (finally) gotten ahead in life.

Not one for lounging, she rolled out of bed and headed for the shower, thinking about her daughter again. Virginia would be returning from a rare visit to her dad's later this morning. Deanna hoped that this visit would be the beginning of more frequent visits to Bernie's. She wasn't sure what had prompted it, but it had given Deanna the freedom to pursue her fling with the hunky billionaire next door.

If it ever did happen, Deanna was under no illusions that her relationship with the bad boy next door would be anything but a glorious roll between the sheets. Her failed relationship with Bernie, the philanderer, had taught her to keep everything with men purely physical and fleeting. Clay was not the kind to put down roots. When he'd accomplished his mission in Panama City Beach, he'd be on to another lucrative challenge somewhere else.

*So what?* Deanna thought, scrubbing off beneath the pulsing rain shower. *That just means I'll get another fat commission for turning this condo over again. Win-win!*

Deanna wondered idly how all this moving affected his eight-year-old. She sympathized with Clay as a single parent, but considered whether Clay's single-minded attitude toward his work left his son with a lot of time spent with nannies and babysitters. She shrugged. Virginia had had sitters and nannies after they'd moved to Panama City Beach. She'd turned out just fine.

For a fleeting moment, Deanna wondered whether the celibacy her daughter had adopted had anything to do with the multiple couplings of her parents.

*Did that part of our lives affect her too? How can a girl reach twenty-two and still be a virgin?* Deanna wondered, reaching for a nearly-empty bottle of shampoo. *Is that normal?*

She gave up that train of thought as she soaped up her long hair, still almost completely naturally blonde, and began to think about various meetings she had scheduled for the day.

4
---

## CHAPTER FOUR

Virginia balanced parcels and reached out to swipe the card in the elevator. It dropped on the floor and she muttered, "Damn!"

"Here. Let me get that for you!" a deep voice said. Over her packages, Virginia saw a tanned hand reach around her to swipe a card in the slot.

"Thank you!" Virginia peered over the top of her boxes—way over the top ...wow, he was tall—into the deepest, bluest eyes she had ever seen. "Hi," she squeaked. *I sound like a school girl,* she thought. *Not like a twenty-two-year-old, master's-level college student.*

"Can I help you with those?" asked the man, taking two boxes from her.

"Thanks," breathed Virginia, flexing her fingers where they tingled from brushing up against his. "They're brochures for a program at Gulf World. I have to fold them so they will be ready for Monday," she explained.

"And you're ...dropping them off here?" he asked, nodding at the now-open door to her mother's apartment. "Deanna said something about her little girl working at Gulf World. I didn't realize Deanna herself was involved in volunteering."

"She's not," Virginia said in confusion. "I am. I mean, I'm not. A volunteer. I mean …wow." She had a tendency to get tongue-tied in the best of circumstances, but this was impressive even for her. Stepping past the gorgeous guy, she walked over to a brand-new coffee table and set her two boxes down, then walked back for the others.

He held them slightly away, eyebrows raised in a playful challenge.

She tried again. "I'm Virginia. Deanna's daughter. I work at Gulf World. And you're …"

"Clay. *You're* Deanna's little girl?" There was more than a hint of disbelief in the man's tone, making Virginia laugh even as she processed the fact that this was the hunky billionaire her mother had been ranting and raving about for days.

"That's right. I'm finishing my master's in marine biology." *So eloquent, Virginia. God.*

"Not that I would ever question a lady's age, but …"

"I'm twenty-two," she replied, taking his boxes from him. "Yes, I know, I'm not exactly little. Mom loves to describe me that way. It makes her feel maternal or something."

"I'd debate the not-little thing," Clay answered, leaning against the door jamb, long legs stretched out in front of him in a way that stretched his jeans just *so,* raising Virginia's virginal pulse several notches. "You're, what, one hundred pounds soaking wet?"

"You don't get to ask a lady both her age and her weight three minutes after meeting her," Virginia retorted, grateful to find that her elevated hormone levels weren't completely tying up her vocal cords.

"Touché." He smiled, and Virginia damn near melted into a puddle on the floor.

Turning away to get a grip back on reality, a reality where this vision of a man was probably doing the horizontal tango with her mother and didn't have any interest in her own skinny self at all, Virginia rambled on, "My mom said something about you having a son?"

"Yeah. He's six and a huge fan of marine life." He followed her into the living room and eyed her as she opened one of the four boxes, examining the brochures with a critical eye due to her need for distraction from how close he was standing. She reached under the table, pulled out a drawer, and extracted a mango-flavored Ring Pop. At Clay's amused look, she shrugged. "It's my favorite candy. Doesn't much matter what people think. Want one?"

"Sure," he replied, surprising her. She offered him a selection and he chose lime. Clay took a brochure from her hand and triggered the same electric reaction all over again, so that Virginia had to mentally scold herself from taking a step back.

*Grow up, Ginny. He's not interested and he never will be.*

"Does he live with you?" she asked, fumbling for some kind of basic poise, if not at least some fundamental conversational skills.

"He will soon," answered Clay, sliding the Ring Pop into his pocket—not that there was much space, given how snug those jeans were!—doing a neat trifold on the brochure, and putting it aside, then reaching for another. "He's finishing school in Houston, then he's moving in. His only request was that we live on the ocean."

"Maybe he'd be interested in coming to see the dolphins," Virginia suggested, suddenly inspired. "I run the Swim with the Dolphins program. I could get him into the summer volunteer program," she added. "It's a lot of clean-up work, but he'd be around amazing marine animals and dedicated staff."

He folded another brochure and gave her that killer smile.

"That'd be wonderful. Wait until I tell him. There's only a matter of logistics. I leave for work early and don't get home until dark. But I'll figure out something."

"I could take him to work with me and watch him until you get home," Virginia offered.

*What's gotten into me?* she wondered. *Yeah, he's smokin', but I barely know this man!* She sensed that women flocked to be helpful around this gorgeous, single dad with the rippling muscles.

"Will your mom mind?" he asked, working his way steadily through a tall stack of brochures.

She struggled not to stare at his nimble fingers or wonder what they'd be like doing something far more interesting. "Probably not," replied Virginia. "Let's not play games. She wants you."

Clay looked up from the paper and grinned from ear to ear, utterly unaware of the affect that full-wattage smile had on Virginia. "Yeah. But don't worry. I'm behaving."

She swallowed and almost fanned herself with one of the folded glossies. "That's unusual around my mom. She's gotta be off her game."

"I don't think so. My interests just ...lie elsewhere," Clay murmured.

Was it her imagination or did he lock eyes with her for a long moment when he said that? Totally her imagination. Had to be, as he started for the door.

"When you come over to meet Parker, I'll give you the number for a person who can donate a machine that will do all this folding for you. There are so many other fun things you could be doing ..." With a slow, sexy wink, he vanished into the hallway.

Exhaling a long breath, she collapsed back onto the pillows. *Did that really just happen??*

5
---
## CHAPTER FIVE

"You're sure you don't mind?" Deanna's voice was slightly slurred over the phone line.

"Of course I do. We were all set for a movie night and you're ditching me for some hot guy in a bar," Virginia replied. "But you do you. You always do."

"Don't be like that ..."

Only drunk Deanna cared much about whether Virginia was offended. Sober Deanna would chalk it up to whining or attention seeking.

"Have fun, Mom. Make sure he uses something. Night." Virginia hung up the phone and stared at it for a second, shaking her head slightly. She had a decent relationship with her mother, but sometimes it felt so ...weird to be the one having to remind her parent to use condoms.

With a sigh, Virginia opened her laptop and signed onto Skype. In an instant, the beloved, geeky face of her best friend, Arty Stone, appeared. Arty stared myopically at the screen and pushed his dark-rimmed glasses up on his nose. Virginia noticed with amusement that Arty's glasses were taped together with adhesive tape and his pocket bore the splotch of an uncapped, blue Sharpie. And he needed a haircut. Arty just never seemed to get around to those life practicalities.

*Some things never change*, she thought happily. She could always count on Arty to be the stereotypical computer nerd and brilliant scientist he was.

Virginia had met Arty years ago in a chat room for kids with dysfunctional families. His parents had already been legally separated and her parents had been in their pre-divorce stage. She'd been pretty sure her dad was having an affair, and they'd fought all the time. Somehow, she and Arty had made it through the rough years together and had come out stronger in the end, still close friends.

A bit of an insomniac, Arty could always be counted on to respond to her Skype requests day or night.

"What's wrong, Ginny?" he asked, skipping the pleasantries and cutting to the heart of the matter, as was his habit. "You've got that scrunched face thing going again. Mom madness or Dad dick moves this time?"

"The weekend with my dad was surreal," Virginia admitted, setting up beside the laptop with a bunch of brochures. "It's so weird having someone draping herself all over him, and she's, like, my age. Then, I arrived home and made a fool of myself in front of the billionaire next door."

Arty nodded in sarcastic commiseration. "Billionaires will do that to you every time."

"Speaking of doing it …"

"Your mom wants him?" he guessed immediately. "No surprise."

"Actually, yes, surprise. He's resisting."

Arty's dark eyebrows shot all the way to his hairline. "I think I like him."

"I know I do," Virginia groaned. Thankfully, she and Arty had never had anything but friendly feelings toward one another, and he was actually in a long-term relationship with a great girl, who not only put up with Virginia as his digital 'side piece,' but who saw everything in him that so many other women had overlooked.

Arty smirked. "Hot?"

"As a blue flame."

"Ouch ...how old?"

"He's not old enough for the cougar lady!" Virginia said.

"Did she do the little girl routine? Don't answer. Those eyes say it all."

"Why can't she just be normal?" she sighed. "She got all pissy when she found out I offered to get his son into the Gulf World kids' program. Even though—"

"She volunteered you first," he interrupted, nodding. "Called that one a mile away. So, what's Mr. Blue Flame like?"

"He's donating a machine so I never have to fold these anymore." She held up a brochure.

"Nice. And ... "

"And I did my usual tongue-tied thing. Worse than ever. You'd think that I'd never even kissed a guy!" Virginia wailed.

"Bob behind the bleachers didn't count," he teased, having been her listening ear all through high school drama, as she had been through his. Then he sobered. "Just ...listen, Ginny. This guy may be having a thing with your mother, but he may also have designs on you."

She almost spat out a slug of Mountain Dew, barely avoiding showering her pile of brochures. "Suuuure," Virginia laughed. "Arty, the guy is a god. As in, Mt. Olympus. And, while he may be turning me into Mt. Vesuvius, he's not about to look down from his high home and notice me."

"You always sell yourself short," he remonstrated, holding a hand up as Vanessa called to him off screen, including a faraway hello to Virginia. "One sec."

"Hi, Ness," Virginia called back, folding away industriously and cursing as she gave herself a paper cut.

Arty reappeared a moment later. "Her brother has a flat tire. We've gotta go help him out."

Obviously, he wasn't going to let the love of his life drive around in the middle of the night by herself. Virginia stifled her self-pitying jealousy and waved. "I get it. Be safe."

"Be careful around the guy, Gin," Arty warned again. "You're the one who needs to be safe."

"Go be an amazing boyfriend," she deflected, waving goodbye and cutting the connection.

## 6
## CHAPTER SIX

The massive bedroom in the Seattle high-rise apartment overlooking Puget Sound was dimly lit by the late-afternoon sun sparkling off the water. Bernie cast loving eyes upon the nubile body of his long-time assistant, Lila Black.

"You're the best, Lila, honey," he sighed. "Sometimes, I think I'd have gone mad if it hadn't been for our afternoons together. Why didn't I marry you?"

"Probably because we'd have made each other miserable," Lila responded with a laugh. "We have a better arrangement, Bernie. You pay me well for my in-the-office and in-the-bedroom assistance," Lila said, patting her pudgy boss' bald head. "You bought me this lovely condo. Your bark is worse than your bite, Bernie. I'm probably the only one who knows you're not the horn dog you make yourself out to be to please those insatiable, bored housewives who hang on your every Dr. Bernie word."

Bernie was about to suggest they have another quick afternoon delight when the phone rang. "Who would be calling here at this time of day?" Bernie groaned.

"There's only one person I can think of," said Lila, handing him the phone.

"What do you want, Deanna?" asked Bernie, picking up the phone.

"That's a pleasant greeting," she noted dryly. "Did I catch you inside your secretary? No. Don't tell me. I really do NOT want to know. I'm just calling because a potential customer is your devoted fan for some reason I don't understand, and you owe me several thousand favors. Put him on your show."

This was how they'd operated ever since their divorce, biting hard at each other, but offering small favors every now and then to offset the pain.

"What's in it for me?" he asked, pulling Lila back down and nuzzling her delicious neck. Her soft sounds of appreciation got him going quickly again, something good for his middle-age ego as much as anything else.

"Publicity. Obviously. My prospective customer is wealthy and insane."

"Done," Bernie agreed, rolling over and wrapping around Lila. "Still hot-to-trot for the bad-boy billionaire next door?"

Deanna's voice dropped several degrees, warning Bernie he'd overstepped the boundaries of their fragile non-relationship. "Go to hell, Bernie. And take the woman in bed with you … with you."

She hung up the phone.

Lila met Bernie's eyes and they both laughed, although Bernie's laugh was slightly worried. He reached for his phone, pulled up a picture of Deanna's new customer, and showed it to Lila. "Clay Booth. You think my daughter might fall for him?" He'd worried about Virginia ever since her last boyfriend had smashed her heart to smithereens, not that he'd been around when it had happened. Father of the Year wasn't an award he'd ever win.

Lila whistled. "Yes. Yes, I do. Any idea if he's a good guy?"

Feeling slightly jealous at Lila's reaction, Bernie put the phone aside and kissed her hard. "Virginia is so naïve. So damn trusting. No idea where she got that quality." He enjoyed drawing hungry moans from his assistant, trailing his lips down her ample chest and lingering on all the spots he knew she enjoyed.

"I can talk to her," Lila moaned, head falling back. "Warn her. You and Deanna will never get through to her, the way things stand between you. But Virginia and I get along."

"Thanks, babe." He showed his gratitude by draping her legs over his shoulders and diving in.

## CHAPTER SEVEN

*Calm down. Breathe deeply. It means nothing*, Virginia chanted to herself as she sprinted up the walkway and then was forced to wait impatiently as the elevator took six years to come, then another ten to carry her up to the penthouse floor.

*I should've just run. But then I'd have been a sweaty mess*, she grumbled to herself, stepping out and checking her hair in the mirrors that lined the hallway.

Clay had called her a few minutes back, saying Parker had arrived and asking if she wanted to meet him.

To be fair, Virginia did want to meet the boy, who she was sure was a great kid, but her primary interest was unabashedly in getting a little more facetime with Clay, whom she'd barely seen since their first awkward hallway meeting.

Stopping at his door, she extended her hand to ring the bell, only to have the door swing open before her fingers quite made contact. A slight boy with hair and eyes very similar to Clay's peered up at her.

"Are you the girl who swims with dolphins?" he asked immediately.

"That's me, yes. Hi, Parker. I'm Virginia," she replied, trying not to overtly look around for Clay.

Parker grabbed her hand and towed her inside, where she almost collided with Clay. As Parker spouted off facts— "Did you know that dolphins and orcas are from the same family? Dolphins eat other fish. Did you know there are forty different types of dolphins?"— she and Clay exchanged an amused look and he mouthed, '*Hi.*' Just watching his lips form the words made her skin heat. He was wearing a surprisingly worn T-shirt, not something she'd expect in any billionaire's closet, and the way its soft fabric molded to his broad chest left her mouth dry.

"As a matter of fact, I did know that." She fielded Parker's questions, all the way trying to think of how to silently flirt with Clay, when she barely remembered how to verbally flirt. It had been so long since she and Darren had split. "Did you know dolphins are as smart as apes? Their brains look a lot like human brains. Here's another interesting thing: Dolphins have great eyesight both in water and out of it. They hear ten times as well as humans, but they can't smell."

"Really?" Parker said. His already-wide eyes were suddenly as big as saucers. "Did you hear that, Dad?"

"I'm old, but I'm not deaf," Clay teased, ruffling Parker's curls and earning himself a "*Daaad!*"

Smiling at the warm, normal interaction between the two, so unlike her own relationship with her father, Virginia asked, "Parker, would you like to come and see my show? I'll let you swim with the dolphins. And if you're free this summer and it's okay with your dad, you can be a summer volunteer at Gulf World."

Parker lit up like a Christmas tree. "Are you for real? Can I, Dad?"

The way Clay clapped his son's shoulder left Virginia warm in a different kind of way. There was a solid trust between the pair that made her feel weirdly privileged to witness it. Of course, she'd think of normal family interaction as intimate. She'd never had any.

"I think she's for real, son, yes. And, yes, it's fine with me."

Parker suddenly launched himself forward and wrapped his thin arms around her waist. He squeezed so hard, she let out a startled *Oof!* Parker drew back sheepishly and looked up at her, wreathed in smiles. "Thank you, Virginia. I'll be the best volunteer. I'll even clean up garbage and fish buckets."

He took off at a full run down the hall, maybe to call someone, or maybe to look up more dolphin stuff. Who knew? Virginia stared after him, as touched as she was a little bemused. Suddenly, a pair of far larger arms encircled her from behind and she found herself drawn backward into a very large, muscled chest.

"Thank you," Clay whispered, brushing his lips over her cheek. "You have no idea what that meant to him."

"You're welcome," Virginia managed to mumble, in spite of the total chaos that had erupted beneath her skin. The man felt even better than he looked, and that was saying something. "He seems like a great kid."

Clay's lips lingered where they'd first skimmed over her skin. "I won't forget this. One of these days, I'll find a way to say thanks."

He had no idea that he already was, over and over again, as Virginia closed her eyes and just reveled in the moment before it was broken by Parker careening back down the hall, phone in hand. He didn't seem remotely disturbed by Clay hugging her, and Virginia wondered if that was because Clay had so many women over.

The thought chilled her a little and she drew away, thinking of her father and his many affairs.

Clay gave her a curious look before turning his attention to

Parker's phone screen, where he had some kind of dolphin picture pulled up.

## CHAPTER EIGHT

"Hi, Arty. Oh, ouch." Virginia grimaced at the wisps of toilet paper on his chin where he'd cut himself shaving. "What are you doing shaving at night?" she asked, settling into a comfortable chair she'd dragged out to the balcony after a long, blissful beach afternoon spent with Clay and Parker.

"I'm taking Vanessa out for our anniversary," he replied. "In ..." he glanced at his wrist for an imaginary watch. "Five minutes. So start talking. What's up?"

"Who said there's anything up?" she asked, feeling that stupid flare of jealousy again. Arty had always been 'hers.' If she needed anything, he was always there, at any time. Lately, he'd been less and less available. Virginia shut that absurd, uncharitable train of thought down fast. Of course he was busy. He was building a life with Vanessa.

"I can read you better than I read code," Arty said. "What happened?"

Saying the words made her feel ridiculous, like a teenage girl all over again. "Clay hugged me. And ...sort of kissed me. On the cheek, I mean. Not like a real kiss. Oh, my God, I've reverted to high school, haven't I?"

"More like middle school," Arty confirmed, looping a tie around his neck and beginning to fumble with it.

"Twice around the tree," she reminded him automatically, a veteran of various tie wars since Vanessa had entered both their lives.

He fumbled the knot anyway and had to start over. "I told you. The guy's into you."

"It was just a thank you kiss," protested Virginia. "It meant nothing."

"He knew exactly what he was doing. That innocent neighbor, single father act is just a ruse."

"You're being ridiculous, Arty!" protested Virginia. "Clay IS my neighbor and he IS a single father. How can that be a ruse? And a ruse for what, for that matter?"

"To get into your pants, obviously. Ginny, you may have miraculously gotten over Darren, but for both our sakes, I don't know about this guy. Be careful."

"That's right. You don't know this guy," she retorted, stung at his mention of Darren when they had a tacit agreement that he was never brought up. "What do you mean, for both our sakes??"

"Just be careful, Gin." He got up and peered down at the camera, looking weirdly good in an apparently-new tux. "How do I look?"

"Oh, my God," she realized abruptly. "You're— "

"Shhh!" Arty frantically motioned her silent. "Yes. I'll tell you all about it later. For now, just do me a huge favor and be careful, Virginia. Much as I love you, I may be a little busy to sweep up pieces of broken heart this time around. Wow. That sounded like a total dick, huh."

"Total," she agreed, wiping her eyes and smiling. "But merited. Go get the girl, Arty."

His round face furrowed and he leaned in closer. "Talk to Lila," he urged. "She may need to be the new me, if things go well tonight."

"Oh, Arty." She sat up and beamed at him, in spite of the selfish heartbreak she was feeling. "There'll never be a new you, and things are going to go great tonight. Lila already called and warned me away from Clay for the same reasons you are. I've got someone watching my back. So stop worrying about me and go pop the question!"

He smiled then, his face suddenly as innocent with joy as Parker's had been earlier. "Love you, Gin."

"I love you, too," she said softly, watching her best friend walk off the screen and knowing that an era in her life had just come to an end. Reaching for her as-yet untouched glass of champagne, she raised it. "Here's to you, Arthur Stone. You've left middle school behind for good." She couldn't help the treacherous thought that lingered at the back of her mind—*so where does that leave me?*

Her melancholy fled as she realized something of absolutely vital importance, making her lunge for her phone.

*TAKE THE TOILET PAPER OFF YOUR FACE!!!!!!!*

## CHAPTER NINE

Even though they'd been visiting the same exhibit first thing in the morning for a week, Parker remained as mesmerized as he'd been on the first trip. He leaned as far over the stone ledge as Deanna would allow him and stared at the furry creatures diving in and out of the water just a few feet away. She rested her hand lightly on his back, not even wanting to countenance what it would be like to tell Clay she'd let his son fall into the seal exhibit.

"Did you know some seals have ears and some don't?" he asked. "Seals have thick fur and blubber to keep them warm," he added. "And seals spend most of their time in the water, but they mate and have their babies on land."

Virginia responded automatically with a fact of her own. "And did you know that seal milk contains a lot of fat and their babies gain three to five pounds a day?" All the while, she was lost in her own thoughts. In the weeks since Parker had arrived, she'd managed to steal ten minutes here, even a few glorious thirty minutes there, with his father. Every now and then, she got the impression that he might be equally smitten. But then he'd go entire days where it seemed like he was avoiding her.

Like today, when he'd apparently had to rush out to a meeting five minutes before she'd arrived.

"And polar bear hair isn't white," Parker informed her. "It's clear. The snow makes it look white."

She smiled and made a show of digging up another obscure marine biology fact, although, in truth, she was running out, what with Parker's surprisingly extensive knowledge. His interest in the subject matter went way beyond the normal kid interest in all things furry.

They made their way through the facility, stopping at the pool with the brand-new baby orca. Suddenly far more subdued, Parker pressed his hands to the huge pane of glass and stared at the tiny creature.

"Where is its mother?" he asked quietly.

Unsure about his change in tone, Virginia said, "We think she might have been killed. Some fishermen brought her baby here."

"I don't have a mom, either," Parker said solemnly.

Her heart went out to the kid. Her relationship with her mom might be fractious—she'd seen Deanna twice in the last week and both chance encounters had ended in fights—but at least she had a mother.

"Do you miss her?" Virginia asked, thinking immediately that it was a stupid question. But Parker didn't seem to mind.

"I was too little to remember her when she went to heaven. But, sometimes, I remember things. I remember lavender," he said. "It reminds me of my mom. Do you miss your dad?"

Tentatively, she put her arm around his waist and was surprised when he immediately leaned in. She squeezed him lightly. "It's ...not quite the same. My dad lives a long way off, but I can still visit him—if I want. He and my mom fought a lot when they were together. It used to frighten me. I thought that if they hadn't had me, they would have been happier."

Parker burrowed closer, his voice muffled.

"I thought if they hadn't had me, my mom wouldn't have died."

She swallowed back a lump in her throat.

"I'm sure you had nothing to do with her death, Parker. Sometimes people just get sick."

"I'd like a new mother," Parker said. "Then my dad wouldn't be so sad and stay away at work so much."

"Maybe, someday, you'll get one." She guided him away from the tank, considering what exhibits might help restore his previous happy mood.

"She'll have to love my dad too. My dad says we're a package deal." He stopped beside a jellyfish tank and squinted at the long tentacles.

"Of course you are. Hey, bet you can't tell me how big an octopus' heart is ..."

## CHAPTER TEN

The scene was just too tempting. Clay walked in and spotted Parker ensconced in a recliner, avidly devouring what was obviously a brand-new dolphin book. He lifted a finger to his lips as he walked past, warning his son to be silent as he walked into the kitchen. He'd smelled the heady fragrance of basil and tomatoes all the way from the hall.

Finding the beautiful Virginia standing at the stove, her hair curling at the ends from the steam, Clay stopped and just appreciated the view. Her tight jeans framed her firm backside like a canvas. Not a surprise, given that Clay had pretty much decided the woman was a work of art, far beyond just the physical. The way she seemed to genuinely enjoy his son; her total disinterest in Clay's money; her lack of any kind of artifice ... he'd found himself drawn more and more to her in the days since they first met, to the extent that he'd eventually started manufacturing excuses to stay away.

Losing Louise had left him cold inside for half a decade, and all the sex in the world, with the hottest women, had done nothing to warm Clay until Virginia walked into the complex carrying too many packages. His reaction to her had been so strong, so uncharacteristically blunt, when he typically played a long game, that he'd wimped out and tried to keep from seeing her to avoid having the attraction deepen any further. But that was proving increasingly impossible because of Parker's growing relationship with Virginia. They drove back and forth to work together, and it was obvious that Parker was starting to see her as a sister, if not a second mom.

Virginia derailed that dangerous train of thought by calling out suddenly,

"I've never cooked with pans this nice before. I'm afraid to get them dirty!"

"But they have to get dirty for us to taste the deliciousness inside," Clay rumbled, enjoying making her jump.

She spun, dropping a spoon on the floor and splattering red sauce on the immaculate tile. Clay grinned at her wolfishly. Reaching down, he picked up the spoon and slowly licked the sauce off.

"Deliciously dirty," he murmured, dropping the licked-clean spoon into the sink.

Virginia's cheeks, already a light pink from the heat in the kitchen, flushed darker yet. She grabbed a paper towel and bent to swipe up the sauce, but Clay stopped her.

"The cook doesn't clean," he said quietly, deliberately keeping her soft hand in his for as long as possible before crouching to wipe up the small mess.

"Did he scare you?" Parker hollered from the living room.

His interruption didn't break the spell. If anything, it seemed to only intensify the simmering electricity.

"Completely," Virginia yelled back, shaking her head in playful remonstration at Clay. "Welcome home, Mr. Booth. I hope you like lasagna with homemade sauce. I gave your chef my recipe and he had it simmering all day."

That wasn't the only thing that had been simmering, Clay thought to himself. "It smells insanely good. What's in it?"

"That's a secret that only your chef and I share," she informed him with a delightful smirk that made him want to kiss it off her full lips.

"Dad, did you know dolphins can't smell?" Parker appeared in the doorway, book in hand.

"I remember you telling me that once, Parker," responded Clay. "How sad for them that they can't smell our delicious supper." *Or the deliciousness of Virginia's perfume. God. She's practically edible ...*

"Maybe it's just as well," commented Parker. "I gave them their dinner today and it smelled pretty bad."

Chuckling, Clay reached out to ruffle his son's hair and had his gesture summarily ducked as the kid headed back into the living room. He refocused his attention on Virginia, who was bent over, checking the lasagna in the oven.

Clay had never been one to beat around the bush, and in spite of his reservations about starting anything with someone so obviously innocent, his baser desires took full control.

"Keep doing that and I'm gonna have to cancel Parker's nanny's night off."

She slowly closed the oven door and turned, brushing back a wayward curl. "Clay ...what are we doing here?

The sudden vulnerability in her eyes hit him like a gut punch. "Virginia—"

## 11

## CHAPTER ELEVEN

"Hello!" Deanna Matthews walked into the kitchen and beamed at the startled pair. "What a surprise! I come home to spend an evening with my daughter, after being roundly scolded for ignoring her, and discover that she's absconded to our new neighbor's kitchen. Hits you right here, I tell you." She cupped the underside of her left breast, and Virginia flushed to the roots of her hair.

"Mom!"

"What?" Deanna asked innocently, wandering over to peer at the bubbling pot on the stove. "Where did you learn this, missy? You've never cooked for me."

"I will from now on," Virginia promised. "And I'll lace every bite with—"

"Love," her mother cut in cheerily, hoisting herself onto a kitchen stool and kicking her legs beneath the flimsy fabric of a dangerously short dress.

Virginia fought down a surge of atypical anger—she'd long ago accepted that her mother simply wasn't ...motherly. However, tonight, she was feeling territorial for some reason.

"Daaaaad!" Parker's yell came from somewhere in the back of the huge apartment. "I need you for a sec!"

Clay gave Virginia an apologetic look and slipped away, leaving her alone with her now-grinning mother.

"Throwing ourselves at the rich neighbor boy, are we?" Deanna inquired archly.

"Me? Throwing? I'm about to throw something, all right," Virginia warned. "I'm not the one who walked in here and hitched that dress halfway up her thigh!"

Deanna had the grace to flush very slightly. "Can you blame a girl for trying?"

"Maybe not a girl. A grown woman? Yes!" exploded Virginia, waving a wooden spoon and feeling vaguely stupid for doing so. "You're my *mother*. God, I wish sometimes you'd act like it!"

Clay chose that moment to walk back in. "Parker's got an upset stomach," he informed them. "Deanna, can you do me a huge favor?"

Virginia's mom lit up. "Anything at all."

"Can you watch him for a few minutes while I run out to the drugstore?" He nodded at Virginia. "I need her to come with me because I don't know this neighborhood yet and I let my driver go for the night."

To her surprise, Deanna didn't try to flip things around so her daughter was the one who stayed. "Sure," she agreed. "Do I need to do anything for him? Make him ...tea, maybe?" She looked a little lost suddenly and Virginia was more certain than ever that Deanna didn't even know how to boil water. She was far from a helpless blonde when it came to business, but household matters were another matter altogether.

"No, I just need someone here for a few minutes while I run out. We should be back in fifteen minutes. Thanks," Clay said gratefully. "Virginia? Sorry, I should've asked instead of assuming. Do you mind ..."

"No," she said hurriedly, wiping her hands on a towel and nodding at the oven. "Not at all. Mom, watch the lasagna. If it burns, you don't get to eat any." She kissed her mom on the cheek and followed Clay toward the elevator. "Is Parker okay?" she asked worriedly. "He didn't eat anything weird while we were out, honestly."

Clay touched a finger to his lips and didn't say another word until the elevator door closed behind them.

## CHAPTER TWELVE

No sooner had the doors closed than Clay dropped the front. He let the elevator go a few floors and then pulled the emergency stop, stranding the two of them between floors.

"Parker's fine," he told Virginia. "He needed me because he wanted me to 'rescue' you."

She looked adorably confused. "Rescue ...?"

Clay shrugged. "The kid's either going to be a marine biologist or a psychologist someday. He picked up right away on how your mom was bugging you, even if he wasn't in the room. He told me that I needed to give you a few minutes of 'space' so you and your mom didn't fight."

Her jaw dropped slightly and Virginia stared at him for a long moment before laughing. "Wow. I knew I liked your son, but this just took that to a whole new level."

"What about me?" Clay asked, aware his voice was slightly husky as he took a step toward her. "Any chance you like me, Virginia?"

"Um."

His eyes widened, and Virginia's did too. "No, no! That's not what I meant! I like you, Clay. I like you a hell of a lot!"

Relieved that he hadn't completely misread everything, he moved another foot closer to where she was backed into the corner. "So 'um' has a whole new meaning tonight for me, I guess."

"Uh ..."

Grinning, he moved forward again, and then again, until he was directly in front of her, looking down into Virginia's lovely face. "Um and uh. Got it. Is there a new word I should know for, 'is it okay if I kiss you, Virginia?'"

She licked her lips. "Oh."

Clay extended a hand and drew her gently into his chest. "*Oh* is good," he murmured, threading his fingers through her hair and stroking a thumb over her soft cheek. "I've been fighting this ever since I first met you, you know."

"No. Did not know," Virginia mumbled, lightly resting one hand over his on her cheek and sending sparks throughout Clay. "Hoped, though. Really sort of completely. Totally. Hoped."

God, she was incredible, from head to toe and everything in between, including her innocence. "I held back because I'm good at games. I'm not good at relationships. And you seem like a relationship type. Am I right?"

She blinked and suddenly lifted on her tiptoes, resting her palms high on his chest. "I may be out of practice, Mr. Booth, but I think I still remember that kissing involves a lot less talking." Tilting her head, she brushed her lips over his mouth.

He reacted without thinking as heat flared in every inch of his body. Yanking her hard into him, Clay didn't so much kiss as plunder Virginia's mouth. He'd intended to tease and taste the softness of her lips, making love to them before proceeding, but her small gesture fried something deep inside his brain. Tangling one hand in her long hair and resting the other firmly on her backside, Clay delved deep into her mouth, not stopping until their tongues were wrapped around one another and her taste was filling his senses.

"Mmm," Virginia whispered, adding to the repertoire of sounds he knew he'd carry away with him to bed tonight.

Clay slid the hand in her hair down to her neck and cupped it, tilting her head slightly to give him even better access. "Virginia," he whispered, sipping, nipping, and licking at her soft, sweet mouth. "You taste like a dream."

Her response was to nip playfully at his tongue before kissing away the tiny sting. "You taste like my lasagna sauce," she whispered, smiling into his eyes.

He laughed and rested his forehead against hers, stealing kiss after kiss until her lips were deliciously swollen and they were both breathless. "Baby," Clay groaned, his jeans getting tighter every time she skimmed her hands over his shoulders or her lips stole away to sample the stubble at his jawline. "I should've given us more than 15 minutes ..."

"We'll need medicine!" she realized, pulling away abruptly and leaving him feeling bereft.

He drew her back into him, taking a turn at tasting other parts of her beside her lips, like the luscious expanse of her delicate clavicle, the firm line of her toned bicep, the outside of her full breast, working upward steadily until his lips brushed the taut nipple through her shirt and she moaned.

"I've got the medicine covered," Clay promised, sliding his hands beneath her shirt and skimming his fingertips over her soft, bare abdomen. "I want to have you covered, Virginia. Covered by my body as it presses you into the mattress. Any chance you're interested?" His palms glided upwards, paralleling the pull and tug of his lips on her firm nipple through the fabric.

"Yes," she gasped, grinding her hips painfully into his, so it was all Clay could do to avoid stripping them both down right then and there. "But—"

"I don't like buts," he warned, tugging her shirt collar back and laving the tender skin beneath it with his tongue. "I'm crazy about you, Virginia. I want you to give yourself to me. I want to take everything."

"It would be everything," she whispered, so softly that Clay raised his head at last, relinquishing the taste of her delicious skin and exchanging it for what he saw in her eyes, confirming his suspicions.

"It's okay if you're a virgin, baby. No sin waiting to find the right guy," he said tenderly, brushing his lips softly over hers, like he'd originally intended.

"Are you saying you're Mr. Right, Mr. Booth?" she asked, holding his gaze steadily.

Normally that kind of a question, playful or not, would have sent Clay running for the door. But Virginia was different. In spite of the literal door closed behind him, preventing any form of escape, Clay found that he didn't want to walk away. He hadn't been able to all these weeks, as he fell harder and harder, and he definitely couldn't now. Nevertheless, he had to be honest.

"I don't know," he admitted. "My track record with relationships is 1-0."

She nodded, smoothing the hair back from his face and leaving her hand cupping his cheek. He turned his lips into it to kiss her palm. "Parker told me about his mom."

"Parker's crazy about you," Clay replied, for once not feeling a knife stab of pain at Louise's memory. "And if I'm not there yet, I'm pretty close, Virginia. I know it's insane, given that we've spent a total of maybe two hours together so far, besides this evening."

"Then sign me up for Bedlam. I'm close to crazy myself," she said with disarming candor. "It terrifies me, Clay. I got hurt pretty badly a while back. My friends are warning me far away from you. Your reputation as a womanizer precedes you on every newsstand tabloid."

He opened his mouth to protest, and she closed it with a soft, sweet kiss. "But. And you'll like *this* but. Somehow, I don't believe half the crap I glance at while I'm waiting in a checkout line. Not about you, anyway."

He breathed a sigh of relief, but had to ask. "Why?"

"No idea. Just a gut feeling." She lifted his hand and pressed it to her flat abs. "And I'm planning on going with it."

"Who hurt you, honey?" Clay whispered, kissing her slow and hungry, pulling her in flush with his hard body once more.

"I'll tell you about it someday," she whispered back. "But right now, we have like five minutes, I think. I don't want to spend them talking."

He smiled. "I can take orders every now and then. Just one quick thing. Well, two. First of all, I want to thank you for how kind you've been to Parker. He told me you're helping him come up with a PowerPoint on dolphins to present to volunteers. That's ...amazing. And second, I've been asked to go to New York next weekend for business. I'd like you and Parker to go with me." When Virginia looked skeptical, he rushed on to explain. "I'll rent you your own room. You will be responsible for Parker while I'm at meetings and making presentations. So, you can look at it as a job, if you want. The rest of the time, we three can do tourist things. Have you ever been to New York?"

When Virginia shook her head, Clay added, "Neither has Parker. It's a fabulous city full of interesting opportunities. I'd like to show them to you. Will you think about it?"

She was silent for so long that he grew afraid. Then a smile touched the corner of her lips and spread outward until it filled not only her lips and cheeks, but her eyes. "Um." She winked, and Clay's mouth crushed gratefully down on hers, making the most of every last second before they were forced to break, run down the hall to get the drugstore delivery from Clay's driver, and return to the apartment.

As they walked back inside, it was with the greatest reluctance that Clay released Virginia's hand. She smiled up at him, a hint of shyness back in her eyes. "Maybe …my hotel room can be an adjoining suite? Connected by a door to yours, I mean?"

If Deanna hadn't walked into the room at that moment, Clay would have picked Virginia up and carried her straight to bed. As it was, he spent all of dinner—during which a valiant Parker continued to pretend to be sick, so Clay had to sneak him lasagna and have a conversation with his son about how deception really wasn't a good thing—shifting uncomfortably in his seat, longing to be able to hold Virginia close again.

Even with her mom right there, the more she talked, laughed, and listened, the more he realized she had lit up his world when he hadn't even known it was dark. And he made himself a promise that he would not let that light go out again anytime soon.

## 13

## CHAPTER THIRTEEN

"What are we going to do?" asked Parker, almost bouncing impatiently in their hotel suite's luxurious living room.

"It's a surprise," Virginia teased him. "But you need to get dressed quickly."

As Parker flew into his room, she stole a moment to answer Clay's text from ten minutes back. He'd only just left for a full day of meetings, but already, it appeared, he was distracted.

*If I say I shouldn't have brought you with me, it's only because I'm looking at gorilla of a guy who is spouting numbers and he's weirdly reminding me of you.*

She smiled from ear to ear and wandered through the unbelievably plus Plaza suite, texting back.

*I could be offended, but I choose not to be. If I say I'm going to miss you today, is that too much, too soon?*

The response was instantaneous. *Not soon enough. I'll beat you too it. I miss you already, Virginia. How long has it been? Three weeks?*

She popped into the bathroom and eyed the enormous

shower and double bath, seemingly built for at least six. *Since we met? A month and six days. But I'm not counting.*

*Damn. It's like you've been part of my life, and Parker's, forever. Baby, I want so bad to keep texting, but I have to go.*

Fingering one of the plush towels and imagining them wrapped around her naked body while Clay ogled her from the doorway, Virginia grinned.

*Go make more billions. Xxx*

"I'M READY!" Parker shouted, darting past the bathroom in search of her. "Was I fast enough?" he asked, pulling his Gulf World hoodie over his head as Virginia emerged.

"The fastest," said Virginia. "Let's do this, Speedy G."

"Who's that?" he asked, always insatiably curious, as they took the elevator down and walked across the street.

They took the subway to the West 8$^{th}$ Street station. Even the long, underground ride was fun, with Parker chattering a mile a minute and wanting to know more about the cartoon mouse, then examining every inch of the subway and clearly memorizing it for future research purposes.

When they emerged and he realized they were headed for the aquarium, the boy may as well have been candlelit, he grinned so widely.

"Oh, YESSSSSS! Ginny, I love you!"

He bearhugged her tightly, and she pretended that his chokehold was the reason for her damp eyes. Truthfully, she was falling as hard for the kid as she was for his dad. It was starting to feel like they'd always been a mini-unit. A family.

"I know what I want to see first?" Parker dragged her up the stairs and over to the ticket booth, barely able to keep from running off to stare at everything while she paid.

"Let me guess," said Virginia, handing him a ticket. "The sharks and the aqua theater."

. . .

"How did you know?" he demanded.

"Because that's what I want to see too and I know you have great taste!"

When they left the aqua theater about an hour later, Parker was all excited about watching the sea lions. "Did you see them smile at me?" Parker asked. "I'm pretty sure they knew I swim with dolphins. Can we see the sharks next?"

"It's not finished just yet," Virginia told him. "When they have it all built next summer, it will be 57,000-square-feet. You'll be able to see sharks, rays, sea turtles, and lots and lots of fish. The exhibit will hold 500,000 gallons of water."

"That's amazing!" said Parker. "Can we come back when it's done?"

"We'll have to ask your dad," Virginia told him.

"He'll want to come," Parker said confidently. "Ever since you became part of our family, he's *way* more fun."

Virginia coughed and blinked hard. She was putting her heart seriously on the line here. If Clay ultimately decided she wasn't what he wanted ...firmly, she stopped that thought, born solely courtesy of Darren's treatment. Clay wasn't like her ex. Not at all. If he was acting interested, it was because he was. "So ... what do you want to see next?"

"The penguins," shouted Parker.

"Let's check the schedule to see when they feed them. That would be fun to see. Wouldn't it?"

"Can we see them now and come back to see them feeding them?" suggested Parker. "And the seals are right next door. I love seals. They're so funny."

"The seals put on a show, so we'll check to see what times they do that. And then I thought you'd like to see the 4D show at the theater. It's SpongeBob and Friends."

"What's 4D?" asked Parker. "I know what 3D is."

"I'm not sure," Virginia confessed. "I guess we'll find out!"

. . .

THE DAY FLEW by packed with activities from minute to minute, and before long, they had to hurry back to make sure they got back before dark. By the time they reached the Plaza's subway stop, Virginia was half carrying Parker. He yawned and blinked his eyes hard, fighting sleep all the way up the elevator and into their suite. Virginia let them into the room and guided Parker to his room. She disappeared just to go to the bathroom, and when she got back three minutes later, discovered him sound asleep on top of his bed, fully clothed, clutching his new sea lion snow globe.

Gently, Virginia began to ease off his shoes, smiling when Parker muttered a little grumpily in his sleep and tried to turn away.

"Want some help?"

She jumped and looked over her shoulder, catching Clay standing in the shadow of the doorway. "Hi," she whispered, smiling and feeling the by-now familiar warmth move through her. It wasn't just how good he looked—although, good grief—in that bespoke suit that exactly matched the color of his eyes and was tailor-made for his big body. He certainly did look good. But it was just as much the gentleness in his smile as he looked between her and Parker and the feeling that he liked seeing her dote on his son.

He walked over and touched her cheek lightly with his fingertips, but didn't do or say anything else as he bent to help her with his son. Together, they undressed Parker just to the point where he'd be comfortable. Then Clay scooped him up and Virginia pulled back the covers. He gently set his boy down on the clean, cool sheets, and she covered him back up. Parker immediately burrowed down, mumbling something or other about turtles, it sounded like.

They slipped out of the room, leaving the door slightly ajar. As they emerged into the living room, Clay reached out and pulled Virginia tightly into his arms.

"I'm officially falling hard," he whispered, kissing her with a tenderness that she'd thought only existed in the movies. "I love watching you with my son, Virginia. I love going to work and knowing that I get to come home to you. It's way too soon to ask you to move in with me, though. Isn't it?"

Virginia leaned into him, feeling boneless in the wake of his kiss and the emotion in his voice. She wanted badly to agree, but someone had to be marginally adult. Damn it. "I feel the same way, Clay. I mean it. But it's too soon, yes. I don't know if Parker's ready for that yet. Or if we are, honestly."

He sighed and brushed his lips over hers again. "Yeah, yeah. Will you promise to at least consider it in the next month or so?"

"I promise." She slid her arms around his neck, feeling the words on the tip of her tongue and fighting them back.

"You're afraid," Clay murmured, lifting her in his arms and carrying her over to the balcony. "I see it in your eyes sometimes." Pushing open the glass doors, he stepped outside, not letting go of Virginia for a second. "Why, baby?"

He read her with dangerous accuracy. She was tempted to dodge, but if this was really going to become …something …he needed to know at some point or other.

"Remember, I told you? I got hurt," she said quietly, settling into his chest as he set her down and pulled her into him, his arms securely around her waist. They looked out over New York's incredible night skyline, but she had a hard time appreciating it as the memories came rushing back.

"By someone?" There was tension in his voice and it made her twice as nervous about saying anything.

"Yes. You can't go nuts if I tell you this though, Clay. I've dealt with it. I have some trust issues, okay, but so do you. I'm not damaged goods or anything. What's done is done."

"You're not damaged anything," he replied, tightening his hold on her. "Tell me, Ginny. Please."

Her nickname on his lips sounded so much sexier than when Arty had said it.

"I was with a guy for about a year. Somehow it never felt right to ...go all the way. He was patient for a while. Then he got tired of it. He tried to ..." she stumbled over the words. "Force me."

Clay drew in a sharp, harsh breath, telling her that was not what he'd expected to hear. "*God,* Ginny."

The memories were painful, but surprisingly, not as devastating as they'd once been. "He didn't manage it. I fought and screamed and someone called the police. I managed to lock myself in the bathroom until they showed up and arrested him."

He buried his face in her neck and held her so tightly that she could feel his heart pounding behind her. "Sweetheart. Baby. I'm sorry. I had no idea."

"I'm okay," she repeated a little more forcefully, suddenly desperate to make sure he didn't misunderstand. "I have my moments when it's hard to trust a guy, yes, but I'm okay, Clay. Please don't let this change things between us."

He turned her to face him and leaned down to rest their foreheads together. "The only thing it changes is that I'm suddenly adding *brave* to everything else I already know about you. You're right. You're not damaged goods, Virginia. Not one bit." The passion in his words made her tremble as they stared into each other's eyes before his mouth found hers and began a slow dance of tongues and lips, heating her from the outside in.

"Clay," she whispered, holding on tightly and meeting him kiss for hungry kiss. "Please." She didn't even know what she was asking for. Thankfully, he seemed to understand.

# 14

## CHAPTER FOURTEEN

"I won't betray your trust," Clay said huskily, slipping the clip from Virginia's hair and letting her thick, blonde waves tumble over his long fingers. The cool New York evening breeze lifted several soft strands and brushed them over his cheeks and lips.

She stared up at him so openly, so trustingly, that he knew in that moment what he'd been denying all along. He didn't dare tell her yet. Not until he'd given her more reason to believe he was going to stick by her through thick and thin. But the bottom line was, he knew without a shadow of a doubt, that he was in love with Virginia Matthews. The thought was as joyful as it was terrifying.

"I ...got hurt in a different way." Sitting down in one of the balcony's recliners, Clay drew Virginia on top of him, her long legs straddling his waist in a way that tugged a groan from him.

"Parker's mom." Virginia nodded, guilelessly moving over him, clearly not aware that every brush of her hips over his was pushing him closer and closer into orbit.

"Yeah. But not just because she died. She didn't want Parker, Ginny. She wanted it just to be the two of us. She died giving birth several months early because she went to a 'friend' to try to take care of what she considered a problem."

Her eyes widened. "Clay! I'm sorry. I—"

"Shhh." He smoothed his palms over her hips and rocked slightly upwards, watching her face shift as she belatedly realized the effect she was having on him. "I did love her. It made her reaction to Parker all that much harder. I couldn't understand why she didn't want that bond between us. A child is so ..."

"Symbolic. Cementing," she filled in. "I know, Clay. Parker isn't my son, but I know. Honestly."

He nodded. "I know you do." It was one of the reasons, he realized, that he loved her. "I didn't try to force her to have him, I swear. But I didn't just sit down and roll over when she told me she wanted to get rid of our child, either. We fought the entire pregnancy." He shook his head. "After she died, except for Parker, I went numb to the whole world for years. I think I was still mostly numb when you walked in."

Virginia leaned down and kissed him softly. "I'm sorry, Clay."

"I'm not numb anymore, Ginny. Not even a little bit." He lifted his hips again and looked into her eyes, watching them slowly fill with heat that matched his own desire as he rocked back and forth between the apex of her thighs.

She moaned and he kissed her throat, feeling the vibrations move through him. "I've never felt like this. Not even with Louise," he whispered, nibbling down the deliciously soft skin. "It's like you turned me back on—" Her laughter made him grin. "Yes, like that. But in other ways too. I'll have to tell you all about it later. Right now ...I'm going to feast."

"Feast?" she repeated, a hint of nervousness appearing in her tone again.

He soothed her with a tender kiss. "Only if you want me to." Gently, he cupped her full breasts and looked up into her eyes.

"You're beautiful, Virginia. Beautiful and warm and delicious. I want to taste you from head to toe, and everywhere else in between. Like this." Leaning up, he brushed his lips over the hint of exposed cleavage beneath her modest blouse.

Her head fell back and she moaned again.

"Is that what you want too, honey?" Clay murmured, repeating the light kiss and promising himself that he'd go as slow as she needed, no matter how much his body screamed for mercy.

"Yes," she whispered, reaching for his hand and lifting it to her again, molding his fingers over her soft curves.

"You're in control," he told her, as he began to slowly undo each frustratingly small button. "You say stop and we will. Immediately. No questions asked."

Holding her gaze, torturing himself deliberately till the last second, Clay didn't look until the two halves of fabric fell apart. Then he slowly lowered his head and took in the incredible sight inches away from his lips. Virginia's beautiful, full breasts were cupped in a simple, white bra with a hint of lace. No lingerie had ever been sexier, he thought, fighting the urge to devour.

Instead, he drew her back to him and began a slow exploration, listening to the cadence of her moans and whimpers, reveling in each sharp intake of breath as he tasted and touched, lifted, and gently squeezed, and gradually peeling back each cup inch by inch until his lips were directly on her skin.

"Clay ...Clay ...*oh, my God, Clay,*" she called his name again and again as he fulfilled his promise of feasting, licking and suckling and nibbling and nipping in concentric circles until he finally reached one taut nipple and suckled hungrily.

She cried out so loudly that he would have been afraid Parker would hear if they hadn't been outside and he hadn't known how soundly his son always slept. "You like that, baby?"

Hearing her almost come undone just from his rapt sucking made Clay borderline frantic. He groaned into her skin, working to push away the remainder of his clothes and hers. "Ahhh, Ginny ...touch me too," he urged, discarding his shirt so violently that it might have gone over the balcony—not that he cared.

Then her shy hands and lips were exploring his bare chest, and Clay would have lost it completely, had he not been so in love with this delicate, precious woman. If he'd had any doubts, his desire to take care of her pleasure first more than confirmed his feelings.

"I love your lips on me," he murmured, sliding his hands up beneath her skirt and stroking their rough palms over her thighs. "That feels so good, honey."

Taking obvious pleasure in his reaction, she bent closer to the task, working her way down his pecs to the taut line of his abdomen. When her tongue darted out and traced the firm ridges of his six-pack, Clay saw stars explode behind his eyelids. When she dragged her fingers playfully up and down his bare skin, following each light scrape with her lips, it was all he could do to grip the sides of the chair and let her be the one in complete control. And when she slowly, carefully eased down the zipper of his suit pants, well, heaven stopped being somewhere high above and came home to rest squarely in his arms.

"*Aaaaah*," he gasped as her soft hand tentatively enclosed his hard shaft.

She jerked back, and Clay reached for her hand frantically. "No, baby. It's good. So good. Please." He wasn't ashamed to beg as he folded her fingers around his rigid erection. "Please, touch me, baby. Oh, God, yes ...*yes.*"

"Show me how," Virginia requested, looking up at him shyly through a curtain of windblown, blonde hair. "I want to do it the way you like it."

"If I liked it anymore, I'd be embarrassing myself like a teenage kid," he promised, nevertheless reaching back down and guiding her small hand beneath his own in a firm, pulsing rhythm. "That's ...right ..." he managed to gasp out as she got the hang of things. "Oh ...yeah ...so right, Ginny. Use your free hand too, baby. Like this." He guided her left hand to his balls, drawn up so tightly they ached. "Be real gentle," he urged, drawing her down into a passionate kiss, his tongue imitating the thrusting motion of his hips. "Oh, Ginny. Ginny ...Ginny ..."

It was clumsy, first-time, youthful sex as she tried different things, every single one of them wringing another pleasurable groan from Clay, and he'd never had it so good, not with a single one of his well-experienced one-night stands.

When he absolutely could not take it anymore, after she'd experimented by taking him between her lips and he'd had to recite baseball stats to avoid terrifying her by thrusting violently, Clay somehow managed to disentangle them enough that he could lift her. He kissed her all the way down the long hallway to her adjoining hotel room.

Laying her down on the bed, he covered her with his naked body like he'd promised to in the elevator and pulled her back into a searing kiss. She wound around him artlessly, not playing any games and giving herself utterly to him, and somehow that gave Clay make a tiny measure of control.

"You're the most beautiful person I've ever known, naked or clothed," he told her huskily, earning a low laugh.

"I'm addicted to you, Clay Booth," she said simply, pressing a kiss to his shoulder and running her fingers once more against his rampant erection.

He shuddered and nudged her back. "Not just yet. I have one more place I want to feast." Somehow, he managed to take his time covering her in kisses all over, drawing out both their torture and enjoyment, until he reached the juncture of her thighs. Then, drawing her long legs over his shoulders, Clay met Virginia's eyes.

"I've spent so many nights dreaming of doing this." Then he dove into her soft, sweet depths and drank from her like a starving man, her instant cries breaking past his desire to go slowly and driving him right to the brink of insanity.

"Never tasted anything so damn sweet." He groaned again and again, burying himself in her tender folds and finding new meaning for the word *feasting*.

Her thighs clamped tight around him and Virginia grabbed for a pillow, muffling what was obviously a wild scream. "CLAY!"

She bucked and writhed as he continued to lap deeply, opening her very gently with first one finger, then two, giving her all the time she needed to adjust to the new sensations. And she gave herself to him completely, without a single reservation, coming so hard that the large bed shook.

It was almost as good as coming himself.

"I can't wait anymore, Gin." Clay finally rose above her again, watching her pleasure-hazy gaze follow him as he settled his painful erection between her legs. "I want you all the way. Are you ready for me, honey?"

"I've been ready," she rasped, cupping his cheek in one slightly trembling hand. "You're not the only one who's had to take cold showers the last month, Clay. I've spent plenty of nights doing anything but sleeping. Let's just say ...my vibrator hasn't seen that much action in years."

This time his kiss wasn't nearly so soft as he met her lips ravenously. "You undo me," he growled, easing forward into her unbelievably tight, warm body. She tensed at the intrusion, and he bent his head to suckle her breasts until she slowly relaxed again, shuddering once more with pleasure. "That's my girl. You're mine, Ginny. All mine." *Nobody else's ever again*, Clay vowed to himself as he kissed her hard and thrust deep, swallowing her slight cry.

"That's the only time it'll ever hurt," he swore, fighting the urge to move hard and fast now that he was so deep inside where he'd always wanted to be. "Ginny, you feel better than any dream. I can't not tell you anymore. I'm sorry if it's too soon. I love you, baby. I'm hopelessly, completely, wildly in love with you."

Her eyes misted over, then, and she smiled slightly, moving her hips into his. "I love you too, Clay. But you have this habit of talking too much when other things need to be happening."

The words on her lips nearly made his own eyes gleam. Instead, Clay concentrated on sweeping them both away to a shattering climax that ended just as another one started. They made love throughout the night, sleeping for brief stretches, then reaching for one another once more. It wasn't until Virginia couldn't ignore how sore she was any longer that Clay insisted they stop. Then he held her long past sunrise, reveling in the perfection of her body against his, until he was forced to slip away to make sure he was in his own bedroom before Parker woke.

## 15

## CHAPTER FIFTEEN

"There she is!" Parker hollered, stabbing a finger at the Statue of Liberty. "She's 305-feet tall and named after the Roman goddess of liberty! WOW! She really *is* green!"

Standing behind the excited kid, Virginia and Clay held hands loosely. They'd tried it casually while walking through the Met earlier in the day, and Parker hadn't objected at all. Now, Clay wrapped his fingers more securely around her cold ones and lifted them to his warm lips, drawing her closer to his side.

As Parker rambled on, Virginia melted into Clay, resting her head against his broad chest and wondering if all of this was just one giant dream. They'd been in the city less than forty-eight hours and Clay had apparently decided that he had enough money. He'd ditched his meetings and had joined her in taking Parker every place his young boy's heart had ever dreamed. In between places, she and Clay had managed to steal warm, soft kisses every time his attention was turned away. Sometimes they were a little less than soft, edged with hunger on both their parts and the desire to return to the hotel suite.

She still ached from the night before, but no force outside of an eager, young boy wanting to see the whole world would have kept Virginia from repeating it all over again with Clay. It was still hard to believe that last night hadn't been just another fevered dream, but it couldn't have been. Nothing she'd ever imagined had come close to how Clay had taken her apart and put her back together again, in the best possible way.

"Virginia Matthews ..." he whispered in her ear, teasing her with a light earlobe nip.

"Hmmm," she whispered back, returning the tease by sliding her hand underneath his T-shirt and scraping her nails over his taut skin.

He swallowed an audible groan. "I just like saying your name."

"Feel free to use it anytime." They were about the cheesiest pair ever, she'd decided. But the fact that they *were* apparently a pair made up for any cheese. Clay seemed to be relinquishing his fears of another broken heart, and Virginia ...well, Darren was all but forgotten.

"Dad, did you know there are almost ten million people living in New York City? And it's over three hundred square miles. New York is actually five boroughs. It's called The Big Apple, but no one knows why."

"You should figure out why, son. If anyone can, it's you."

They made their way through Liberty Island, Ellis Island, and Rockefeller Center. By that point, the sun was starting to set and, stuffed full of New York pizza that he'd proudly consumed "like a local"—crust first—Parker was a bright-eyed, yawning zombie. They tucked him in bed, then escaped to the farther bedroom to do everything they'd been dreaming about all day.

## CHAPTER SIXTEEN

Virginia was positive she would never get used to the luxury of traveling with a billionaire. Because of his notoriety—which he freely admitted he'd gained from being a bad boy with plenty of tabloid conquests—the only way Clay got any kind of privacy was to travel by private plane. He didn't go in for *total* excess, not usually at least, he told Virginia, so it was a small charter plane, rather than a massive gold-plated jet.

Still, the fact that he owned his own plane, *any* kind of plane, was astonishing enough for Virginia. It was crazy convenient not to have to book tickets or try to figure out flight dates. One moment they were in New York, the next Clay decided they were going to go see his parents.

"Parker hasn't seen them in a while. And I want them to meet you," was his simple explanation that morning as they made love in the shower. "We may not be moving in together yet, but it's going to happen sooner rather than later, Ginny. I want you. I need you. Always." His lips came down on hers and her legs wrapped around his lean hips. All conversation ended.

A few hours later, they were in Chicago, driving a rental to his parents' place. It took all of five minutes for Virginia to feel totally at home with the couple, both retired neurosurgeons. Clay's intelligence was apparently genetic. They enjoyed a long, homemade dinner, then gave Parker the chance to spend an evening with his grandparents while Clay spirited Virginia way, under orders from his dad to show the little lady a good time.

"I don't have anything to wear," she protested as he casually informed her they were going on a dinner cruise.

"Will you get mad if I say I've had that covered since we left New York City?" he inquired playfully, jabbing a thumb at the bag in the backseat.

"Mad?" she repeated, eyeing the bag uncertainly. "Clay. What did you do?"

"It made me think of you," he promised. "I would've given it to you anyway, trip to Chicago or not."

"Okay ..." A little nervously, Virginia pulled the bag toward her and peered in. "Clay!" she exclaimed, drawing out the shimmering blue dress, complete with a pair of strappy stilettos. "You ...went shopping for me. Wow. That's. Uh. A little *Pretty Woman-ish*, maybe."

He winced. "That's not how I intended it. That's kind of unfair, don't you think? I haven't done anything to treat you like a whore."

It was Virginia's turn to wince. "Ouch. No. No, you haven't. I'm just ...a little overwhelmed," she had to admit. "In forty-eight hours, I've had sex for the first time, admitted to being in love, flown on a private plane, been told by your son that he wants me to be his new mother—"

"*What?*" Clay veered off the road abruptly and killed the engine on the shoulder. "What did you say Parker said?"

She blinked, surprised again. "It happened this morning, after I made him toaster waffles and before we caught the plane.

You were on a business call, I think. He hugged me hard and said he wished I could be his mom."

Clay's eyes held an expression she'd never seen in them before—one she couldn't read at all.

"And when were you planning on telling me this?"

Virginia shook her head, bewildered. "I don't know. When I thought about it? I wasn't keeping secrets, Clay. Like I said, things have just been moving really fast, and I guess I was trying to absorb everything."

"Right." His tone, at least, she could read. It was cold. Frigid, actually.

"You're acting like I did something wrong," she pointed out, feeling like she was getting emotional whiplash. "What's happening, Clay?"

He looked away, glaring out across the mostly deserted road at the Chicago night. "What's happening is that I tried to do something nice for you by getting you a present and you tell me I'm treating you like a prostitute. Then it turns out my son apparently has designs on you as his new mommy, but you chose not to share that with me."

A sick feeling started in the pit of Virginia's stomach. "That's not how any of this happened. I didn't mean—"

"You didn't. Maybe. But it came across that way."

It felt like she'd been slapped. Who was this cold stranger? Abruptly, Virginia realized what a fool she'd been. She knew next to nothing about Clay Booth. She'd let herself be carried away by her fantasies and now she was neck-deep in a situation she'd hoped to never be in again, having her heart broken. Not that Clay was doing anything like what Darren had, of course. But his sudden coldness made her ache all the same, like he'd attacked her heart, if not her body.

She unlocked her door and shoved it open.

"Where are you going?"

Ignoring him, Virginia stepped out into the warm night. Even so, she rubbed her arms as she started walking aimlessly.

"What are you doing?" Clay caught up with her a moment later, grabbing her arm.

Virginia wrenched away. "I think we both made a mistake," she said as calmly as she could. "It was all too much, too soon. I feel like I don't know you at all, and I'm realizing, it's because I actually don't."

If she'd hoped he was going to see how unreasonable he was being and suddenly go back to being the Clay she'd fallen in love with, she was sorely disappointed. "You know who I am. I've been honest from the first day. I'm a playboy, Virginia. A *bad* boy. I've been through my fair share of celebrities. And prostitutes. Maybe that's why I knew what dress to pick."

The urge to slap him hit hard and she took a step back. Even as he spoke, a change came over Clay and he suddenly looked uncertain.

"Whoa." He raked a hand through his hair. "Ginny—"

She shook her head. "Please don't call me that. Don't follow me. Just—don't do anything. I feel like I can't breathe." Hurriedly, she walked away once more, fighting back a wave of brokenhearted tears.

"Virginia," he called after her. "I'm sorry. God. I'm so sorry. I don't know what the hell just happened. Please. Give me a second chance."

"Not on your life," she replied tersely, marshalling anger to avoid weeping. "I'm nobody's play toy. Not sexually. Not emotionally. I don't know what game you thought you were engaging in, but I'm out. I am so out, Clay. Goodbye."

She continued to walk down the deserted street, scanning hopefully for any sign of a cab. Behind her, she half-hoped, half-dreaded hearing Clay come after her, but there was no sound. About a block down, a yellow cab emerged out of the darkness and she flagged it down, grateful she'd kept her wallet even though Clay had been paying for everything.

"The airport, please," she said, climbing in. She closed the door and rested her face against the cold glass, still reeling. Over and over again, her mind played the same broken record with only a three-word lyric: *What just happened?* Another, more insidious tune played behind that one, in Lila and Arty's voices. *Be careful. He's a bad-boy billionaire who thinks he owns the world, Virginia. Watch your heart.*

## CHAPTER SEVENTEEN

"What did you do, Dad?" Parker asked yet again, looking as distraught as he had when they'd arrived back in Seattle several days ago. "Why did she leave?"

Sprawled on the couch, one arm over his face, Clay tried for a coherent reply when his head felt like he'd had ten too many drinks, even though he hadn't touched a drop. "It's complicated, son."

"Then uncomplicate it," his son pleaded. "I miss her, Dad."

*I miss her too. God, I miss her so much.* He'd made himself a promise weeks ago never to let the lights go out that Virginia had turned back on in his life. Then he'd somehow carelessly thrown it all away and snuffed out candles, light bulbs, halogens, and LEDs, so that now he was stumbling blind in the dark.

"Dad," Parker insisted. "DO something. Fix it!"

"I don't know how, son," he admitted wearily. "She won't answer any of my messages."

No small wonder why. Clay was still trying desperately to understand how everything had fallen apart in the span of minutes. One second he'd been wildly in love, literally carrying a ring in his pocket because he couldn't wait any longer to beg Virginia to spend the rest of her life with him. The next, he was following at a careful distance, afraid to get too close for fear of watching her literally run away, but not about to let her wander Chicago's streets alone.

"Say you're sorry. Whatever you did, just apologize."

"Sorry doesn't always work, Parker. Do me a favor, son. Go read a book or something, okay? I'll take you out to dinner later. Right now ...I just need to think."

There was a broken exhalation of breath and Clay groaned as he realized that he'd made his little boy cry. And there was nothing he could do to fix that, either, as Parker shuffled out. Virginia had made it blatantly clear that she wanted nothing to do with him ever again. Who could blame her?

*What did I do?* He wondered yet again, replaying the entire mess of a five-minute scene over and over in his head. Why had he reacted that way? What the *fuck* had gotten into him, for him to rake Virginia over the coals like that? She'd deserved none of it.

And then—to top it off—he'd gone and made things even worse. Not that there'd been the slimmest chance that Virginia would have forgiven him. But just in case, it hadn't helped that, when she'd knocked on his door to ask for her suitcase full of clothes—she'd apparently assumed nobody would be home and that she'd only be talking to the housekeeper—Clay had had one of his old ...friends over. A friend wearing nothing but scant lingerie.

The look of disgust on Virginia's face as Marla had opened the door had been enough to tell Clay all hope was completely obliterated. She was never going to listen to him try to explain that they hadn't done anything. He'd just invited her over. Why? Just ...because.

"What is wrong with you?" Clay muttered out loud, rolling off the couch and stumbling toward the kitchen.

The doorbell rang and he change directions, heartbeat abruptly racing. Parker ran out of his room, eyes full of hope. "Get it, Dad! I bet that's her!"

"Oh, son. I doubt it." Nevertheless, Clay almost jogged to the door and yanked it open. His small hope vanished like a blown-out candle flame as he looked at an unfamiliar, stocky guy with a round, reddish face. "May I help you?"

"You'd better," the man said bluntly, shoving a set of taped-back-together glasses high on his nose. "I may not look like I can do much damage, but I can create a virus that will destroy every company you've ever created with no trace."

Clay frowned. "What are—"

"My name's Arty. I'm Virginia's best friend. And you're going to fix her, or I'll fix you," the nerdy guy informed him simply, walking straight into the apartment and kicking the door shut behind him. "Nice place. Hi." He directed the greeting at Parker, whose shoulders were slumped again, his eyes brimming. "You must be Parker. Don't worry, kid. Arty's on it."

He turned to Clay. "I heard her side. Now it's your turn. I hope, for your sake, that you're honest with me."

The notion that this weird-looking shrimp of a guy was actually threatening him would have been comical if Clay had had any sense of humor left at all. "I thought Ginny said you were getting married," he commented, following Arty as he walked straight toward the kitchen, like he knew the apartment.

"Don't call her that. And I am. Fortunately, my fiancée knows and understands the place that Virginia will always hold in my life. I'm assuming she told you about me?"

"Yeah. Sure." Virginia had told him all about Arty, as a matter of fact. Clay would have been jealous, if she hadn't made it so abundantly clear that they were utterly platonic. "How do you know where you're going, by the way?"

Arty glanced at him and smirked. "I hacked your security system, dumbass. I know where every single thing in this place is." He veered into the kitchen and hopped up on the same barstool that Deanna Matthews had perched on a little over a week back.

So much had happened since then ... "Give me one reason I shouldn't call the police."

"Virginia. If she has any love left for you, it won't last if you throw her best friend in prison."

*Shit.* That was a pretty damn good reason, Clay had to admit.

"Start talking," Arty commanded, reaching for an orange and beginning to peel it methodically. "Don't leave anything out. The more data you give me, the better I can program some kind of a solution to this mess."

## 18

## CHAPTER EIGHTEEN

Bernie and Deanna exchanged worried looks over the first cocktail they'd shared in over a decade.

"I've never seen her like this," Deanna told her ex, wearily stirring her drink with a swizzle stick. "After Darren, she was broken up, of course. Devastated. Halfway destroyed. If you hadn't had all kinds of therapy contacts, who knows if she would've gotten the help she needed. But the way she is right now …it's different."

Bernie nodded, swiping at the sweating bald spot on his head. "We did this to her in a sense, you realize."

"Oh, God," Deanna groaned, drowning her disgust with a giant slug of alcohol. "Here comes the shrink talk."

"She's incapable of having a healthy relationship," Bernie lectured. "Can you blame her? Look at the example we set. How long did it take her to fall wholesale for this complete stranger? The same stranger you were trying to get in bed, no less."

"You don't have to make it sound like that," Deanna protested. "I stopped after I realized she liked him. She did fall fast, but have you seen the man? If I was still capable of those kinds of emotions, I'd have done the same thing."

"The point is that she threw herself into a relationship with absolutely no foundation. So when the few plywood boards beneath her feet were summarily pulled up, she fell straight through."

"You all can stop discussing me." Virginia walked unexpectedly into the room, dressed in an ice-blue business suit, her hair dyed a dark red and done in a stiff chignon. "I'm fine. I don't need more therapy from outside or inside the family."

Deanna gaped at her daughter. "What ...are you wearing?"

"I'm leaving to go back to school tomorrow," Virginia reminded her in a blank, neutral tone, exactly the same kind she'd been using ever since getting back from Chicago. "I'm trying out a new look for my return. Something that doesn't say *walk on me.*"

She pivoted and left the room, clicking away unsteadily in a pair of high heels that looked far more appropriate to something Deanna would have worn.

"Bernie." Deanna stared at her ex. "She's acting like me."

He reached for the remains of her drink and downed it. "Like I said. We led by shitty example. And now our daughter's paying the price, heavily. Cheers."

*Three weeks* **later**

The hollow in her heart just wouldn't go away. No matter how Virginia chastised herself and repeatedly insisted to everyone that she was fine, the hole slashed somewhere inside her chest refused to heal. Throwing herself into her studies hadn't helped. Changing everything from her clothes to her hair color hadn't helped. Trying unsuccessfully to sleep with random strangers on campus hadn't helped. As soon as they kissed her, she felt sick.

Two months. That's how long she needed to maintain her focus so she could graduate *summa cum laude*. She'd just been managing to hang onto her perfect GPA, in spite of the total numbness that had taken over her in the aftermath of Chicago. In truth, she would have preferred some of the rage she'd briefly felt, but it appeared she had no say in the matter anymore than she'd had much of a say in whatever happened in that car with Clay.

Saying his name hurt, whether out loud or in her mind. She slapped her textbook shut and stalked out of the library, proud of herself that she no longer wobbled at all on the high heels. And she'd been right about that much, at least. Her new look had garnered a totally different reaction from people. Whereas she used to be 'cute, sweet, and innocent' Victoria, now she looked the part of someone who could grind the world beneath her heel.

She made her way past the quadrangle and into the Student Union Building, grabbing a paltry fruit salad for dinner. Her appetite had seemingly gone the way of her heart.

"V. Hey, V," a voice called, and she reluctantly turned to answer to the new nickname that she'd picked up since getting back from break. No more Ginny. Nope. V for vixen.

Carrie Amsterdam hurried over and gave her a friendly smile. They'd been sort of friends before break. Ever since, Carrie had been trying to figure out Virginia's new 'thing,' and frankly, it was starting to get old.

"Hey," Carrie said again. "Don't tell me that's dinner?"

"Maybe." Virginia had no interest in conversation. "Need something?"

"Yeah, actually. I'm really struggling with my conclusion to my dissertation. Before you left, you said you might—"

"Sorry. I'm busy."

To her surprise, Carrie didn't do her usual sad shuffle and let her stalk away. Instead, her eyes flashed and she grabbed Virginia's salad away.

"Okay, Lady Bitch. Here's the deal. I don't know where my friend went, but I want her back. Nobody likes this version of you."

Virginia was surprised to find that she almost flinched. Hastily, she tucked her heart further away. "Like I care about that."

"Stop it, Virginia," Carrie snapped. "I mean it. This isn't you."

"You barely knew me before," she pointed out acidly. "You're hardly qualified to—"

Before she knew what was happening, grapes and soggy cantaloupe rained down over her perfectly done hair and over her previously immaculate clothing.

"Come find me when you stop acting like a pouty teen." Carrie strode away as Virginia gaped and tried unsuccessfully to wipe away the sticky fruit juice suddenly coating every inch of her upper body.

"She's right, you know."

The familiar, low voice hit her in the stomach. *No.*

"You can't be here," she said to no one in particular, still trying to wipe herself clean.

"This isn't you, Ginny." Clay's deep voice came closer, making her tremble abruptly.

"You can't be here," she said again, starting to hurry away and finding that she was suddenly wobbling all over again in the damn heels.

Images of red lingerie and huge silicone breasts practically thrusting through the fabric hovered in her mind's eyes as she finally gave up, kicked the shoes off, and did her damndest to walk at lightspeed without outright running.

"I won't leave." Clay's voice continued from behind her,

keeping relentlessly easy pace. "I gave you some space, because that's what Arty and I decided what you needed—"

She spun around, mouth dropping, and even the sight of his unfairly handsome everything didn't affect her, for once. "Arty. *Arty?*"

Clay stopped a few feet away, hands raised and palms out. "He came to me. He threatened to hack every business I've ever had if I didn't listen."

Virginia snorted. "He could do it, too. What do you want, Clay? Because for the record, I'm tired of people deciding what I need. What I need is for everyone to back the fuck off."

"No."

She blinked. "Excuse me."

"No," he repeated. "I gave you some space, but enough is enough. If you really want me to walk away for good, then you have to listen to me this one last time. No interrupting. No running. Just hear me out. Please. If not for my sake—yes, I'm going to shamelessly use my son. You broke his heart too when you walked away without even saying goodbye."

To her dismay, guilt suddenly suffused her as she pictured Parker's eager, little face. And with the onslaught of guilt, her defense mechanism faltered significantly, leaving her feeling open again. Vulnerable.

Clay began talking, as if she'd agreed to listen. "It took me a while to work through what happened in that cab. What I finally concluded—and I'm an emotional rube, apparently, so Arty did a lot to help me get here—is that I panicked. Plain and simple. That dress was a precursor to something else I'd planned to give you that evening. When you didn't seem to like it, I freaked out at the realization that you wouldn't like the other gift either. And then when you told me about Parker and the whole mom thing, it drove home the point even further that I wanted to ask you to marry me, but there was obviously no way you were going to ever find me worthy."

He had to be speaking in tongues, for all Virginia understood of what he'd just said. "I'm sorry. Marry what? Huh? What the fuck are you talking about, Clay?"

"Stop with the cussing, Ginny," he said softly. Sadly. "It's not you, any more than those awful clothes and hair. Yes, you can wear whatever you want, say whatever you want, and do anything you *damn* please. I'm not trying to control you. But I saw the real Ginny. And this isn't her. This isn't the woman I fell in love with."

"Marriage," she repeated, still stuck on that. "You were going to propose to me that night?"

In wordless response, Clay reached into his pocket and pulled out a small black box, holding it out in the palm of his hand.

## CHAPTER NINETEEN

He hated what she'd done to herself in the name of never being hurt again. It physically hurt to see the shell Virginia had tried to hide herself beneath, plastering on makeup an inch thick, forcing her blonde curls into a rigid red bun, and stuffing herself into clothes that suited 5th Avenue business women, but not his soft, warm, easygoing marine biologist.

"I love you however you look. However you talk. If this is who you really want to be, then I'll love that person too, somehow," Clay said quietly, watching her face and finding it difficult to read beneath all the makeup. He still held the ring box in the palm of his hand, watching her watch it. "I get it. It really was all too much, too fast. So let's slow it down, Virginia. Give me the chance to take us back to the very beginning. Please."

"You moved on from me in two seconds," she whispered, tears in her voice giving Clay an odd sense of relief. So she was still in there. The hurt he'd helped cause hadn't erased her permanently.

"I invited Marla over." He nodded. "I fully admit that. I was angry and confused and an idiot. But I didn't touch her, Virginia.

I swear on my son's life that I didn't lay so much as a finger or lip on her. She tried. When you rang the doorbell, she was in full swing. I shouldn't have called her, of course. But I didn't mess up completely."

"How can I trust you?" she asked plaintively, wiping her eyes and smearing mascara every which way. "You promised not to hurt me, Clay."

"I did. And I'm sorry that I broke that promise. For the record, you hurt me too. And Parker. That was the part I found hardest to forgive, until Parker himself pointed out that people do stupid things all the time. He insisted that I couldn't stay mad at you just because you made him sad. Leave it to my son to put everything in perspective."

She covered her crimson-painted mouth with her hand, crying harder now. "I'm sorry. As much as you hurt me, I shouldn't have done that to Parker. You're right. I acted like my mom. But that's not an excuse."

"No. It isn't." He shook his head. "We both screwed up pretty much beyond belief. So let's be adults about it and unscrew things, Ginny. I love you. So much. I can't give up on us. I won't. Please." His voice cracked and he flicked open the small box, revealing the Ring Pop—the exact same flavor she'd been sucking on the day they met. "See? We can start again."

Virginia stared at him, and he was vaguely aware that there were other people on campus and that they were out in a very public place, potentially about to cause a huge scene. And then it didn't matter because she launched herself at him and wrapped her arms around Clay fiercely, pressing her face to his chest as the Ring Pop went flying, box and all.

He locked his own arms tightly around her tiny waist, even smaller than it had previously been, and held on tightly. He buried his face in her dyed, fruit-juiced hair and longed for her soft blonde curls, but it didn't matter one bit. Because he had his

Ginny. "I'm not ever letting you go again, Virginia Matthews," he whispered. "I'm just warning you. Officially or unofficially, I'm yours. And you're mine."

She lifted her head and stared up at him, looking such a total mess that he would've laughed if it hadn't been utterly the wrong moment. Then she flashed a watery grin and did it herself.

"I love you. It made me insane to think I'd lost you. I guess I was acting the part, huh."

"Slightly ..." Clay agreed, smiling so hard his face hurt.

"Will you still kiss me, even though I look like a poor attempt at my mom?"

"She did try to seduce me before you showed up in my life," he teased, gathering her closer still and trying unsuccessfully to wipe some of her mascara away with his thumbs. "Maybe she'll enjoy a little of this by proxy."

"Gross," she complained, standing on tiptoe and kissing him hard. "I'm so sorry, Clay. Will you forgive me?"

"And how," he rasped, losing himself in her sweet—even sweeter than usual because of the juice—soft taste, the only part of herself that she hadn't managed to camouflage. "Just don't ever walk away again," he whispered into the hungry kiss. "If you're mad, throw things at me, yell, break windows, anything. But I promise you, Ginny. This is it for me. And I'm going to fight for it, every single time."

"So will I," she vowed, sliding her hands into his hair and returning his kiss until he winced. She grimaced and drew back, waving her acrylic nails that were vaguely reminiscent of talons. "Did I scratch you with these?"

Clay burst into laughter. "The scars will be hidden beneath my hair, so it's okay. Just as long as you keep them above waist level."

She smiled. "I'll consider it ..."

His kiss was equal parts demanding and adoring.

"Hey!" Virginia pulled back. "I just realized something. You've met my best friend in person. Before me!"

It was his turn to smile. "Yes. I did. But I can make it up by introducing him to you right now. Ginny ... meet Arthur. Oh, he brought a friend, by the way."

She looked past his shoulder, and Clay knew without looking that Arty was walking their way, holding an elated Parker's hand.

# SIGN UP TO RECEIVE FREE BOOKS

**Sign Up to Receive Free E-Books and Audiobook Codes.**

Would you like to read **The Unexpected Nanny**, **Dirty Little Virgin** and **other romance books** for **free**?

You can sign up to receive these free e-books and audiobooks by typing this link into your browser:

https://www.steamyromance.info/free-books-and-audiobooks-hot-and-steamy/

Or this one:

https://www.steamyromance.info/the-unexpected-nanny-free/

# PREVIEW OF A BILLIONAIRE'S TREASURE
## AN ALPHA BILLIONAIRE ROMANCE

By Michelle Love

**Synopsis**

When he first laid eyes on her, he knew she was the one. She had brown eyes, wavy hair, and plump lips painted a matte wine red. What first caught his eye was the smirk on her face when the teacher called out everyone's name and she didn't reply. As he watched her, he wondered how she could be bold enough to sit in on someone else's class.

HE WALKED to the middle of the class with his hands behind his back and smiled. You could hear the silent whistles and occasional *oh my god* coming from the female students. All except for her. That was new for this charming older man. She didn't even move her eyes up from her bag to see what was going on. The older man was caught off guard since he was always the center of everyone's attention when he walked into the room. A woman had never not taken an interest in him, so this random student not giving him the time of day made him drawn to her and only her.

"HELLO, ladies and gentlemen. My name is Arsen Lockhart and here's how I became a billionaire novelist", the man announced before the class. As soon as the word "novelist" slipped out it was as though something clicked inside of her brain. Her head popped up immediately and she began paying attention.

LOLA ANDERSON. She was the epitome of stubbornness and ruination. Her only goal was to become a novelist, so she had never had time for relationships, or even friendships. Except for one, that is. Lola had a best friend named Arabella Spencer and they had had an unbreakable bond since middle school. Lola was currently skipping her eight o'clock math class to spend time with Arabella and never expected that there would be a seminar. Who could have known that this one day would be the start of something interesting?

**Blurb**

THEY MADE **eye contact from across the room and from the**

moment he saw her, he knew he had to have her. She bit down on her lip as she watched the much older man walk around the classroom. It was really a coincidence that on the day she had skipped her class a great opportunity like this came about. There had to be a reason the universe pulled them together.

# A BILLIONAIRE'S TREASURE

An Alpha Billionaire Romance

By Michelle Love

# LOLA

I began to feel very drawn to Arsen as he started his presentation. Despite the fact that I was in college, I hadn't met any other guy who had that certain type of confidence he did. I examined the way he walked, with his back straight and chin up, the way he spoke slowly making sure every word was articulate, and the way his eye contact burned holes straight through anyone's head. He was the perfect guy, if I wanted one.

I quickly shook away the lustful thoughts and started to take notes. He went into detail about how to market your novels for the age group you want to sell to, and that's where I struggled with my work—trying to make someone want my book in their home.

Arsen also owned a line of hotels across the country named after himself, The Lockhart. I wasn't interested in any of that, though. The fact that this man was a novelist was really attractive to me. He told us about his daily routine and how strict he was with time for his employees. It showed how ruthless he was when it came to his work. He was stern and didn't play with his work. He was a man who knew what he wanted and got it. What was this feeling? I fanned myself lightly and continued taking notes.

A half hour went by and the presentation was over. When Arsen went around to hand out his business card for whenever we needed to 'contact him,' his smile melted the hearts of all of the female students. I fell victim to this feeling, but I would never let that be known. When he handed me the card, we made eye contact and there was a tingling feeling throughout my body. He winked and I was taken aback, feeling attracted but confused. I guess he noticed because he chuckled and moved on to the next row of students.

"What was that?" Arabella asked, smiling. "He was totally just flirting with you"

I rolled my eyes and pulled my bag over my shoulder. "You're over-analyzing things, Bella".

"You like him!" Her eyes widened with excitement as she stared at me.

I raised an eyebrow, trying to mask my nervousness, and stood up from my seat. "I need coffee," I forced out and left the room quickly.

I'm not sure how a simple gesture could get me to crack like that, but it was strange, and I had never felt that before. I rushed out of the class and straight to the coffee shop to clear my mind. I started to think about Arsen again as I waited in line. His suit was so nice—form-fitting without a single piece of lint. His hair was so dark and his gray eyes were piercing.

"Hello! What can I get for you?" I heard faintly in my head. That confused me, but I ignored it. "Excuse me!!"

I snapped back into reality and realized the barista was trying to get my attention. I laughed softly. "Sorry about that. One large cup of vanilla hazelnut coffee please".

The barista put in my order, then told me my price. As I looked through my bag for my wallet, I heard a familiar voice.

"I've got it, and add another large coffee. Black" I saw a man extend his arm, handing the barista a black card. Her eyes lit up at the sight of him and my body tensed up. All of my feelings from just ten minutes ago came rushing back when I turned to see Arsen standing next to me with a smirk on his face.

"You didn't," I spoke lightly, then cleared my throat. "You didn't have to."

"I wanted to, so I did." He chuckled and took his coffee from the barista, and I did the same. "Let's talk."

My eyes widened, and he chuckled again and walked away to a table in the corner. Taking a deep breath, I followed him to the table and sat in front of him.

"You're not afraid?" I asked.

"Of?" He furrowed his eyebrows.

"Being out in public without some sort of bodyguard or protection. You know ... being a billionaire and all." I took a sip of my coffee and almost moaned as the warm liquid rushed down through my chest.

"I have nothing to be scared of ..." He trailed off, not knowing my name.

"Lola," I stated simply and stuck my hand out to shake his. He grabbed my hand and placed a kiss on it. I heard a girl gasp from the table behind us and I rolled my eyes.

"Too much?" He asked, referring to the kiss.

I shook my head in disagreement. "Girls here are just annoying sometimes, but why did you want to speak with me?"

He smiled and took a sip of his coffee. He licked his lips and that made my stomach full of butterflies. "I saw you taking notes and I wanted to ask you what you thought about my seminar."

"Arsen Lockhart cares what I think?" I questioned and smiled lightly.

"I do." He smiled and drank more of his coffee. "So tell me, Lola, what did you think?"

"I really admire how hard-working and dedicated you are." I pushed my hair back behind my ear. "Actually ... can I interview you the next time you're available?"

"Uh. Sure. What will this interview be about?" He leaned back in his seat and crossed his hands.

"You and what made you want to become a novelist." I stared into his eyes as he nodded.

"I should be free next Tuesday around three. I'll tell my assistant. Don't be late, Lola." And with that, he stood from his seat and left.

I just sat there, not knowing what to do really. I was confused about why he decided to leave so abruptly, but after a few minutes, I shook away the thought and went on about my day. I grabbed my cup of coffee and headed back to my suite, which I shared with Anabella. When I got there, she was sitting on the couch waiting for me with a smile on her face.

"Why are you looking at me like that?" I chuckled and took off my jacket, hanging it on the coat rack.

"I saw you and Mr. Lockhart at the coffee shop! You totally have a thing for him, Lo"

I plopped down on the couch beside her and kicked off my shoes. "Why do you think I have a thing for him? We only spoke for like five minutes." I pulled my feet up and looked over at her.

"That's the reason, Lola! You never give any guy—" I cut her off.

"He's not a guy. He's a man. So what if I talked to him? That doesn't mean I like him"

"You never give any guy or man the attention to even have a five-minute conversation. You're a hi-and-bye type of girl" Anabella smiled. "It's good that you say you don't like him because he's too old for you anyway."

*Too old?* I thought to myself. I'm a grown woman. I can date anyone I want, however old. I mentally rolled my eyes and flashed Anabella a fake, small smile. "Yeah. I guess you're right."

Three days of normal activities went by and it was finally Tuesday. For some reason, I wanted to wear something that would catch his eye, so I decided on a black button down, a black skirt that hugged my waist and hips, and a pair of red heels. I did my makeup neutral with a bold, dark brown lip. I straightened my hair and smiled at myself in the mirror. If this look didn't grab his attention, I didn't know what would.

When I walked out of the bathroom, Anabelle's mouth dropped. "Where are you going? You look so hot!"

"My interview with Arsen is today." I smiled and grabbed my bag from the couch. "See ya' later, babes."

I could feel her watching me in disbelief as I left, but I shrugged it off. As I walked toward my car, a ton of guys looked my way or tried to talk to me, but I only wanted Arsen's attention. I hadn't been interested in a guy since I'd been in college, so the act of developing feelings for someone was new to me. Like learning how to walk again.

I pulled up to his office. It was a place I had always seen, but had never thought to research, since this wasn't the place I was from. When I walked through the huge glass doors, my heels clicked against the marble floors. That sound made me feel bold for some reason and helped me stay focused. I was here for an interview, not to fall into the arms of Arsen Lockhart.

The walls had big, beautiful paintings on each wall. 'The Lockhart' was written on the wall behind the front desk. Although it was a big building, I felt as if I belonged. Like this was the place I needed to be.

# ARSEN

"He's straight through the doors," I heard my assistant say from afar. I turned from my view of the city to see Lola sitting there, looking as beautiful as ever. I was shocked. She looked completely different from the girl with the jeans, sneakers, and ponytail she'd been when I first saw her. I smirked and sat down at my desk.

"Hi, Mr. Lockhart. How are you today?" She sat in front of me with a smile on her face and her notebook in hand. I watched as she opened it and wrote something down. She looked back up at me, confused as to why I was staring at her, but I just chuckled and leaned back in my chair.

"I'm doing great, Lola. How are you?" I stood and walked to the front of my desk, leaning against it. I looked down at her in her chair and finished before she could speak. "Let me guess ... 'I'm doing well Lockhart, and I'm looking very beautiful as well.'" I mimicked her voice and laughed.

. . .

SHE CLEARED her throat uncomfortably and shifted in her seat. "Good. Um. Actually, Mr. Lockhart, I was going to say I'm doing fine." She looked me directly in the eyes with a straight face.

I LAUGHED. She couldn't possibly be serious right now. Who knew she couldn't take a joke? Scoffing, I grabbed a cigar from my desk and lit it. "Well, what are your questions?"

"FOR ONE, I wanted to know what inspired you to become a novelist." She looked down at her book, ready to write. Her nails were painted beige and her hands looked soothing and slightly glossed from the lotion she had used.

"SINCE I WAS YOUNG, I've loved reading, so by the time I was seventeen, I had written my first book. It was never published, but since then, I've been extremely passionate about writing. It's really all I've ever wanted to do with my life, so I decided to turn it into a career. Now look at me—a billionaire!" I laughed and took a drag from my cigar. I loved talking about myself. It's not so much of a 'cocky' thing to do. I'm just very confident, and talking about myself helps remind me of how I made it to the top on my own.

"Great," She spoke, writing down what I'd just said in her notes. "And how long have you been writing, Mr. Lockhart?"

"TWENTY YEARS." I returned back to my seat. "Published my first book when I was twenty-two years old"

. . .

I saw her eyes widen slightly, but she continued to write. Her bracelets clanked together softly and her hair fell on her face. She was so beautiful. I really wanted her in my life. There was a silence in the room and the air grew thick. I decided to lighten the mood a bit.

"How old are you, Lola?"

"'I'm twenty-one, Mr. Lockhart" She kept her eyes on her notes, but I could see her face turning red.

"Do you want to be a novelist?" I asked and she nodded.

She finally looked up at me and spoke. "I do, Mr. Lockhart"

"Call me Arsen," I told her "How badly do you want to be a novelist? How hard are you willing to work for it? It's not as easy as you may think. You can't just write a book and get it published. It's much more than that. It's hard to catch the reader's eye these days, and this field is competitive, since most people read on their electronics. To get to the top, you have to be the best and don't stop working, ever, until you get what you want."

She sat there in shock, not doing anything. She had

completely stopped writing and just stared at me. She was startled and I could see it all over her face.

"Let me mentor you, Lola." I smiled and leaned forward on my desk.

"O-okay, Mr. Lock—Arsen." She shifted in her chair once more and wrote something down in her book. I could see her begin to turn red in the face again.

"Every Tuesday, same time." I stood up and fixed my tie. "I'll show you out"

She looked at me, confused, and stood up, following me toward the door. Before she could fully exit, I grabbed her hand and planted a kiss on it. She furrowed her eyebrows and continued walking.

I couldn't afford to be around her too long or I might just grab her and kiss her. She was so gorgeous, standing at 5'6 with a perfect curvy figure and long, black hair. Her freckles were like constellations and her lips were pouty and desirable. There was no doubt in my mind that she was the most beautiful girl I'd ever seen in my life, and I had to have her. I didn't mean to come on to her too strongly. I guessed that she just needed time to get comfortable around me. She seemed stubborn about who she gave her attention to and that's what attracted me the most. I'd be a fool to let her slip through my fingertips.

## LOLA

He did it again! Cutting our meetings off short, as if there wasn´t work that needed to be done. I rolled my eyes at the thought of it and got in my car. I didn't understand him. The interview was going well until he just went on a rampage about what's it was like being a novelist. I appreciated the advice, I really did, but I didn't expect all of that in that very moment. I definitely didn't expect the kiss he left on my hand before I left. Although that was a very interesting experience, I am happy that he asked to be my mentor. I needed someone like him to help me get where I need to be. The only problem with that plan will be trying to focus on my work with him breathing down the side of my neck. I felt like I was going to melt right in his office, but showing extreme amounts of affection too early with a guy can turn him off or give him the leverage to use you.

When I made it back to my suite, I thought of ways to avoid Anabella, but luckily, she wasn't there. All I could do was lie in bed and think of Arsen. I hadn't felt the weight of a crush in years and it made me feel like an irresponsible schoolgirl again. There was just something about the way he talked. His voice almost struck fear into my heart. Those bold eyes and pink lips. That slender body in that dark suit. I felt myself getting hot and breathing heavily, so I had to quickly take my mind off of the thought of him. I rolled over on my side and pulled my laptop onto my bed. I opened it and the last piece of writing I was working on appeared on the screen.

IT WAS TITLED "DAISIES & APRICOT." It was a short story I had written about my past lover who always brought me daisies and apricot-scented body scrubs. As I read over it, I thought that I would come across some similarities between my ex-boyfriend and Arsen, to give me a little hint as to why I was so attracted to him, but that wasn't the case. Arsen was the exact opposite. He was challenging. All of my past boyfriends were very sweet and submissive. Their personalities fit so well with my dominate behavior. They all fell to my knees the moment they saw me, but Arsen Lockhart was different. He saw me and felt attracted, but he didn't fall to my knees like the rest of them. He remained strong and determined. That's what attracted me the most about him.

I WAS SO USED to being around childish little boys that thought being over the age of eighteen made them "real men," but Arsen was a real man. Strong, hardworking, dedicated, and stern, all while being confident. He had everything he wanted in the palm of his hand and he could control people however he pleased. Except for me, of course. I liked him too, but I wasn't that easy. I was a tough cookie who took a while to be cracked, so if he thought he could have me falling to my knees in a couple of days, he had another thing coming. I smiled, closing my laptop and putting it on my bedside table. I had a man who had my dream job and also had a thing for me. Why not use this to my advantage?

I TOOK one red rose and one white rose from the vase on my desk and carried them to the bathroom with me. I needed some time to relax and to also care for my skin, so I ran a warm bath and added the petals from the roses, pink salt, and a few drops of lavender oil. When I first put a foot in, I felt the warm water kiss my skin and it automatically put me to ease. I played my favorite album on my phone and just relaxed. This was everything that I needed.

I was about three songs in when my phone began to ring. I dried off my hands on a small towel and picked up my phone to see who it was. My eyes widened at the name on the screen. Arsen Lockhart. What was he doing calling me after our meeting? Hopefully it was to tell me why he ended our session so quickly. I hesitated a little, then answered. For some reason, it felt really good to hear his deep voice on the other line.

"HELLO, LOLA," he spoke, not saying anything else.

"HELLO, Arsen. Is there anything I can help you with?"

"I'M TRYING out this new restaurant tonight and I want you to come with me."

. . .

"Well, Mr. Lockhart, I-"

He cut me off. "I'll pay for everything and you can ask me any of the other questions you were going to ask earlier today."

"I guess dinner wouldn't hurt ..." I trailed off and sat up in the tub.

"It wouldn't, so I'll pick you up at 7:30. I'm wearing a navy blue suit, so work around that." And before I could even get a word out, he hung up. I guessed I was going on a date. I sat there genuinely confused and sort of turned on, but I quickly shook off the thought and began to wash off.

When I got back to my room, I looked in my closet and thought to myself, "What do you wear on a date with a billionaire?"

I had to look like arm candy. Arsen Lockhart wouldn't just go out with any girl. It was 6:30, so I just laid out my clothes and started on something else to pass the time. I decided on a simple black dress that hugged my curves, with a pair of heels. I straightened my hair and put on light makeup, but I made sure to wear a bold red lip.

"Where are you going tonight?" I heard Anabella speak from the door.

. . .

"Out," I replied simply.

"Yeah, sure, Lola. Have fun with Mr. Billionaire." She chuckled and walked away. I didn't know what upset her so much about my going out with an older man, but I was a grown woman. If I wanted to date someone much older, I had every right to.

I rolled my eyes at her remark and walked over to the bed to slip on my dress. I felt so beautiful with it on. I never wore it because my mind was too focused on my studies to go on dates. To go anywhere at that. All my life consisted of was writing. I remembered that when I was around eighteen or nineteen, I knew how to balance being a party girl and still getting everything done that I needed to do. That sadly wasn't enough for me, though. I wasn't reaching as much success as I wanted, so I completely cut out partying and having fun at the age of twenty, and here I am today.

I was twenty-one years old and had butterflies before going on a date. There was nothing wrong with that. I just always thought life would turn out differently for me. Maybe that was why I was so open with Arsen. It might not seem like it on his end, but I didn't usually even give guys the time of day, so he was lucky. I felt that he could be that missing excitement that I needed in my life. I was just so used to being by myself without any distractions. I wasn't sure if a relationship was what I needed right now, but I was willing to try it out.

My phone lit up, showing a text from Arsen. It said that he was outside and that his driver was waiting for me. I laughed a little and slid on my shoes. I didn't even know why I expected for a billionaire to drive himself to a restaurant. I made it outside and saw the driver open the back door. I kindly thanked him and got inside. Arsen sat, watching me get in the car with a smile on his face. His teeth were the whitest I'd ever seen. All of his teeth were so perfectly straight that it was mesmerizing.

"You look absolutely stunning," he spoke.

"Thank you. You look good as well, Arsen." I blushed slightly at the nickname he gave me.

The ride there was lovely. I got to see the view of downtown at night, while music played softly in the background. The air was fresh while blowing through my hair. I felt like my nineteen-year-old self again. I heard a chuckle and turned to see Arsen watching me.

"Having fun there?" He smiled.

And for the first time, I actually smiled back. "I am, actually. I'm feeling a bit nostalgic"

"I understand." He nodded. "Go out with me more often and you could feel this all of the time"

The smirk on his face made my stomach drop. "As pleasing as

that offer sounds, I'll have to see how the rest of the night goes before I make a decision"

He shrugged with a smirk on his face and turned to face the window as we pulled up at the front of the restaurant. I waited for the driver to open my door and thanked him after. I looked up at the big, white letters.

"The Crystal Room," Arsen spoke, reading my mind. He grabbed my hand, causing me to tense up and pull my hand away. "It's okay, Lola. I don't bite."

I nodded and he grabbed my hand. "At least not too hard," I heard him mumble as we walked in.

# ARSEN

I watched as her body moved swiftly in that dress. She was the most gorgeous girl I'd ever laid eyes on. I liked a woman with curves, long hair, and an attitude. I was determined to make her mine.

"Hello, Mr. Lockhart. Your table is this way"

We followed the waitress to our secluded table, upstairs on the balcony and took our seats. I ordered us some wine and watched as she looked over the menu.

"See anything you like?" I asked, raising an eyebrow.

"Not really ..." She closed her menu and sat back in her seat. "Order for me."

. . .

I SMIRKED and looked over at the waitress, who had begun to pour our wine into our glasses. "Are you ready to order, sir?" She smiled down at me.

"We are," Lola stated loudly. The waitress jumped a bit from how stern Lola's voice was and I chuckled. She clearly wasn't expecting for her to be that bold. Lola seemed a bit protective over me, but I liked it.

I SCANNED my eyes over the menu and decided on what we were having. "We'll both have the steak and lobster dinner with mashed potatoes on the side."

"C-COMING RIGHT UP." The waitress spoke as she collected our menus and walked away.

"JEALOUS?" I asked Lola as I took a sip of my wine.

"I COULD NEVER BE JEALOUS, sweetheart. Look at me." She smiled and took a sip of her wine as well. "I just don't like being disrespected. I deserve just as much of respect as you do"

THAT TURNED ME ON—THE way she thought so highly of herself. I just wanted to tear that little piece of fabric right off, but I had respect for her. A strong, beautiful woman like herself took time and patience, but I was sure I'd get her to crack soon.

"I WANT to know more about you, Lola. Have you always wanted to be a novelist?" I folded both hands together and leaned back in my seat.

"Since I was about seven, I knew I wanted to write. Every other day I'd try to write a new story or start reading a new book to get inspired. My life literally revolved around it." She took another sip of her wine and licked a drop of it off of her bottom lip.

"There was never anything else you wanted to do?" I raised an eyebrow.

She nodded. "There were, and I did them. I took ballet for a couple of years, I used to sketch, and I'm a pretty amazing cook. I used to want to be a chef as well, but over the years those just became hobbies. I knew I wanted writing to be my career."

"Ballet, huh?" I smiled. "Explains why you have such strong and beautiful legs. I'd love you taste your cooking one day, since you've bragged about your talents"

"You'd be amazed." She smiled and ran her finger around the brim of her glass. "This wine is amazing. So smooth and opulent."

"You want a bottle to take home?" I asked.

. . .

"I sure do." She smiled widely. "Thank you"

Just then the waitress came back with our plates. The food looked absolutely delicious—almost as delicious as Lola. Usually the girls I dated would light up at the expensive meal before them, but it was like she was completely used to this. Has she dated rich, older men before?

I shook the thought and asked the waitress for another bottle to take back home. She politely told me that she'd wrap it up and put it in a bag for us. I nodded and turned my attention back to Lola, who was cutting into her steak. Seeing the fork slide in between her lips after taking a bite made me hot.

"Is the night going well for you?" I asked, staring into her eyes.

"Wonderful," she stated with a smile and continued to eat.

"Maybe we could do this again tomorrow night?"

"Sounds lovely, Arsen, but I'd really like the next time we see each other to be at our next meeting." She poured herself another glass of wine. "I have a lot of work to do and I would love to be undistracted."

"Oh." I cleared my throat. I'd never been turned down. I was starting to wonder if she even liked me. I began eating my food.

. . .

"I would like to do this again, though. She smiled and continued eating.

"Then we shall." I wiped my mouth clean and smirked.

"Arsen Lockhart, I am going to murder you!" a woman screamed as she ran towards me. She began hitting me, yelling that I had killed her husband and ruined her family. Lola was shocked, but managed to pull the lady off while workers rushed over to see what all the commotion was. I dialed my driver's number and told him to be out front of the restaurant immediately.

"I'm so sorry, Mr. Lockhart!" A random woman said to me as she tried to clean off the food that the woman had spilled on my clothes while going crazy. "I'm the manager and I'm not sure why this would happen"

"You should really work on your establishment if you're going to let crazy people like that inside of a place like this." I looked at her, then over at Lola, who was taking the extra bottle of wine from the waitress. I quickly grabbed her free hand and dragged her out of there. We quickly got inside of the car and the driver sped off.

"Um, what was all of that about?" Lola asked.

. . .

"I HAVE NO IDEA. I've never seen that woman a day in my life." I shrugged and turned to look out of the window. I knew exactly who that woman and her husband were, but that was none of her business.

I HEARD her sigh deeply and adjust herself to face the window. She probably didn't want to go out with me again, but I would make sure that she did.

## LOLA

That was one of the weirdest things I'd ever encountered, and the fact that Arsen knew absolutely nothing about the situation seemed very fishy to me. I really loved the feeling of being taken out and shown off, but not if things like that were going to be happening. I wondered if he was hiding something.

"Why do you think she'd do that? Throw an entire fit in front of everyone, claiming that she'd want to kill you in a public restaurant, and why would she accuse you of killing her husband?" I unlocked my phone to text Anabella to tell her that I was coming home and that I didn't have my key.

"Simply because I am a billionaire, Lola. People will do anything to get their hands on my money, even if that means accusing me of false crimes. I don't even have the time to kill some random man." He scoffed.

"I guess you're right," I agreed and looked out of the window the entire ride back. When we pulled up to my dorm, I called Anabella, but there was no reply.

"Let me walk you to your door," Arsen offered with a smile.

"No, it's okay. I've got it." I laughed slightly and proceeded to step out of the car, until I felt him pulling me back by my hand.

"What? Do you think I'm going to murder you or something?" He smirked, staring me directly in the eyes, and I felt my body go entirely numb. His voice sounded so chilling—more serious than playful.

"N-no, you can walk me there," I said quickly, pulling my hand away and getting out of the car fully. I was in such a blank state of mind that I forgot to thank the driver.

"Here's your wine," Arsen said walking around the car and handing me the bag. I nodded with a slight smile, then led him into the building and up to my door. I knocked a few times, but there was no answer. I tried calling a few times too, but there was still no answer.

"I mean, you're always welcomed to stay with me for the night," Arsen offered.

There was a solid ten seconds of silence before I even replied. I had to seriously think, *do I really want to stay with this man after he made several romantic advantages or do I want to sleep outside in the hall until Anabella realizes that I'm here*. I turned to him slowly and laughed. "You promise you won't kill me?"

"I'll try not to." He threw his head back and let out a loud chuckle that made me jump. His arm slid around my lower back and he walked me back outside to his car. The car ride back to his place was long and silent. The only sounds were the wind and soft music playing in the background. I felt like something was going to happen tonight, but I just couldn't put my finger on it.

We pulled into the driveway of his house and it was luxurious. I had never seen anything like it before. There were plants everywhere and I could see the view of the pool upon entering. The driver got out and opened our doors, wishing us a good night, and Arsen led me into his home.

"This place is so beautiful." I looked around at the fiery red furniture and black decor.

"Almost as beautiful as you, Lola. Follow me." He led me to the clear doors of his elevator. "Let's get you into something more comfortable."

"What did you have in mind?" I raised an eyebrow.

"Nothing too serious. My daughter is a little younger than you. She comes to visit time from time, so I always have new clothes here for her to sleep in," he laughed. "She's a little smaller than you, but I don't think there's anything that you can't sleep in"

When we made it upstairs, it was just as huge as the downstairs. There was a long marble-floored hallway that led to what I suspected was his bedroom, because it was the biggest. Upon entering, I saw the biggest bed I'd ever seen in my life with black silk sheets.

"Wait here while I go get you something to put on." He winked and then left the room.

I wasn't quite sure how to feel about that. I was just happy to take these shoes off. I sat on the edge of his bed and kicked off my heels. I found a small hair tie in my clutch and pulled my hair into a high ponytail. I looked around the room and it was very minimalistic, but still very opulent.

"I found this for you." Arsen spoke and my head snapped in his direction. He closed the door behind him and walked over to me. He handed me a champagne-colored silk nightgown. He began unbuttoning his shirt and walking into the bathroom attached to his room.

"Where can I change?" I asked him.

"Right there." He peaked his head out of the bathroom. "Don't be afraid. I won't look"

I heard him laugh as I tried to quickly get out of my dress and get into the new one. When I took off my bra, I turned to see him walking out of the bathroom in only his boxers. Let me tell you, for an older man, he had a great body. I erased the dirty thoughts from my mind and just stared at him.

He looked at the shocked expression on my face and down at my body and smirked. I looked down and noticed that I was only in my underwear. The air in the room became thick and I quickly grabbed the gown to cover myself. I didn't have a bad body, but for some reason, I felt really embarrassed and uncomfortable. I mean I'd only known the guy for a couple of days. It wasn't really the right time to be naked around him, especially when I wanted to wait for this moment if things even got that far with Arsen and I.

"Lola, you don't have to hide from me. We're both old enough to be naked around each other and comfortable with it" He walked by me and picked up my clothing from the floor. He placed them on a chair next to his desk and looked over at me again.

"Where will I be sleeping?" I tried changing the subject to take away from the awkwardness.

"With me, hopefully," he responded. "I respect whatever boundaries you have. I just haven't slept next to a beautiful woman in a long time."

I nodded slowly, not wanting to put up a fight, and climbed into bed. He turned off the light and got into bed next to me. Directly across the room was a huge floor-to-ceiling window and the curtains were pulled back completely. There was a beautiful view of not only the moon and stars, but of the city as well. I could see almost every building that was well-lit and that alone made me feel safe. The light from outside made it easier to see around the room and to see that Arsen was staring at me staring at the view.

I looked over at him and smiled. "The view is beautiful. Thanks for letting me experience this"

"Anytime you want to see it, let me know" He ran his hand over my thigh and it drove me crazy. "You know, Lola, I've wanted you ever since I've laid eyes on you"

"I'm well aware, Arsen," I replied bluntly, trying not to say too much.

"Well, do you feel the same way?" I felt him move a little closer to me.

"Maybe." I smirked and rolled over on my side. I felt him pull me back so that my body touched his and his hand grazed my leg.

"So why aren't we doing anything about that?" His hand slipped between my thighs and I began to melt, but I wasn't going to let him know that he had full control of my body at the moment. I pulled his hand away and laughed lightly.

"Goodnight, Arsen Lockhart."

"I really felt like the connection was there. I guess not." He spoke quietly. He moved back away from me and turned over. "Whenever you're ready, Lola, just let me know"

"Again," I smiled to myself. "Goodnight, Arsen Lockhart."

I woke up to a mist of water on my face. "Wake up, angel."

I sat up and rubbed my eyes to see a woman standing over me with a tray of food. "What was that you sprayed on my face? It feels ... really refreshing"

"Rosewater, ma'am. Mr. Lockhart ordered that we wake you up beautifully with a nice breakfast"

"Mmm." I smiled, closing my eyes and inhaling the smell of pancakes. The woman placed the tray of food on my lap and I automatically dug in. It was like nothing I'd ever tasted before, although it was a simple meal—pancakes, eggs, and bacon with a cup of tea and a bowl of fruit on the side.

"Mr. Lockhart had to leave early for work but he says that you are welcomed to stay here until he gets home. He left you an outfit at the end of the bed and if you are ready to leave before he gets home, just let me know and I'll phone the driver" The woman smiled and left the room without saying anything else.

Who would've expected that Arsen would even let me stay after things didn't go as he planned last night? I guessed he really liked me. I sat the tray of food aside after I was finished eating and slid out of bed, grabbing the clothes that were left for me. I walked to the bathroom and saw the most beautiful shower I had ever laid eyes on. The shower head was the entire ceiling and the doors to the shower were clear with a gold trim. I was in love.

I took off my clothes and hopped inside. I turned on the shower and the water fell down on me like the mist of a rainforest. I looked at the shelf built into the shower and saw all of the beautiful bottles of body wash and shampoo. I helped myself to whatever I needed and got myself cleaned up. I grabbed the two folded towels inside and dried my body and my hair.

After taking the best shower of my life, I put on the dark jeans and fitted shirt that he had left me. These really hugged my body, so I guess he picked them out for a reason. I walked back to his room and shot him a text asking if I could check my email on his computer.

While waiting for his reply, I walked around the upstairs of the house and eventually found his daughter's bedroom. She looked just like him, gorgeous and model-like. I saw why her clothes were too tight on me. She looked around seventeen or eighteen. I wondered if she knew her dad liked girls a couple years older than her. I saw a picture of a woman who seemed to be her mom. I wondered what the relationship was like between her and Arsen and why they weren't still together.

I shrugged away the thought and went to explore more of the house, then Arsen finally texted back and told me that I could use the computer. I continued my exploration down the hall and into another room, which was just full of plants and a different computer from the one in his room. For some reason, I felt the urge to use this one.

I sat at the desk and turned it on. To my surprise, there was no password on it. I logged into my email as an extra account because I didn't know if I should just sign out of Arsen's or not. I clicked through a few messages and saw that classes were canceled today, so that was good on my part. I was going to skip them anyways. I really felt tempted to just switch over to Arsen's account and see what an actual novelist's inbox consisted of.

So I did it. I scrolled through a couple of spam messages and emails for upcoming book events until I saw something interesting. A read message was titled, "I am going to kill you, Arsen Lockhart." It reminded me of the crazy woman from the night before, so I decided to open it to see what it was about.

*"Dear Arsen Lockhart,*

*I knew about this whole little business you and your rich friends were running and I had nothing to say about it because it didn't affect me that much, but you have crossed the line. Michael was a kind, loving man and father of three who was just doing what he had to do to provide for his family, and you go off and kill him? He had a life! Whether he had your stupid drug money on time or not, he still had a life and a family and you took all of that away from him. You took him away from us. Now what are we going to do? He was the one who made a living for us. Either you give me 5 million dollars or I am going to kill you, Arsen Lockhart! I will sabotage your entire drug cartel and make your life a living hell!!"*

I quickly exited out of the email. My heart was beating extremely fast. I knew Arsen was hiding something by the way he reacted last night, but I didn't know that it was a drug cartel. I didn't know that he would actually kill someone! I shut off the computer and stood up. I turned to leave and saw Arsen standing at the doorway.

"Hello, Lola," He said sternly.

# A BILLIONAIRE'S POSSESSION

An Alpha Billionaire Romance

By Michelle Love

## LOLA

Have you ever felt as if time has stopped around you, but in that specific moment you were unable to move? Unable to think and speak clearly. That's exactly how I felt after learning that the man that I was developing feelings for was a murderer, then turning to see that him watching me go through all of his private information.

My heart dropped to the pit of my stomach as I hesitated to respond to Arsen. He raised an eyebrow with a smirk on his face.

"I see the clothes fit you well," he spoke, looking me up and down.

"Hello, Arsen." I finally managed to speak and looked straight past him into the hallway. "Yes, the clothes fit very well. Thank you"

Before I could even make it to the door, Arsen stepped in and closed it behind him. "Did you ... find all that you were looking for on the computer?"

I gulped and nodded. "I'll just be leaving now."

When I tried to walk past him, he grabbed my wrist and I felt myself being pushed against the wall. I gasped and looked up at Arsen, who was now hovering over me. I could tell by the look on his face that I was caught and this wasn't going to be easy.

"You know, it's really not polite to go through people's emails. You don't have the right," he spat.

"I don't know what you're talking abo—" I mumbled and was quickly cut off.

"Don't play stupid with me, Lola. I was standing in the doorway the entire time," he scoffed.

"Arsen, I swear—" I was cut off again.

"I know what you saw on that computer and you don't know how much trouble you're in now, Lola. But you don't seem like the type to be a loud mouth about these type of things, so I'm considering letting you go." After he said that, I felt so much relief. He smirked down at me and backed away slowly. "Just know that if you run your mouth about anything, you'll end up like that woman's husband. Unlike his situation, your family won't have the fortune of ever finding your body."

That was oddly a turn on. Not the fact that he would kill me, but the way he was so serious. Not once did he crack a hint of a smile. His face showed zero emotion, almost as if he was heartless. No man has ever talked to me in that tone of voice and it gave me a bit of a rush. Feeling myself shake in fear and pleasure, I bit down on my lip and nodded in agreement. He flashed a look of confusion as his eyebrows knitted together. He was clearly confused about my reaction. For once, I felt …submissive, and I liked it too.

"Come on. I'll give you a ride home. You can grab your things from the bottom of the stairs." He turned and left the room, and I followed after him like a lost puppy shortly after. It seemed as if the hallway grew longer with every step I took. The tension was so heavy and the air was so thick that I found myself almost out of breath. I fanned myself to try to calm down.

Once we made it down the stairs, I grabbed the bag with my things in them and slid on my heels. They surprisingly went well with the outfit I was wearing. I said my goodbyes to the house workers and went outside to Arsen's car. He was already inside, staring forward toward the view of the city.

I realized that this wasn't some bad boy, good girl fantasy. This was real life and I was actually next to a murderer. I never understood how people could kill one another. It just didn't make sense. I guess it could come down to that sometimes, but from what I had read, Arsen was completely in the wrong. If that's how things were in drug cartels, I was glad I had never become a part of one.

I sat in the front seat and as soon as I closed the door, he sped off. I didn't even have time to put on my seatbelt. He must have still been upset about the situation. Why wouldn't he be? Some random girl had found out his biggest secret. I'd be pretty upset too. There was an awkward silence between us.

His grip on the steering wheel made it painful for me to watch. I found myself constantly switching my thoughts. One moment I was thinking about how amazing it felt to be put in my place and another moment I was realizing how my life was actually in danger at that point. I wasn't sure if I actually had an attraction for this side of him or if I was just romanticizing the situation to make myself more comfortable.

I wondered what he was thinking about. Maybe about the ways he would tell his gang that I had found out their secret, or maybe about how I had betrayed him by going through his personal emails. I guessed I would never find out, because I was too afraid that asking him that might just make him snap. I decided to just leave that situation alone and focus on the city lights ahead of me. They brought me some type of peace in this terrifying issue.

Arsen was so deep into his thoughts that he didn't realize that he had passed my building on campus.

"You missed my building." I spoke a little too loudly. He jumped a little and quickly put the car in reverse, moving back toward my building. I admired his tightened jaw and how straight it looked. His skin was very smooth without any wrinkles. I guessed anything was possible when you were a billionaire. I grabbed my bag and opened the door. "See you tomorrow, Mr. Lockhart."

He finally looked at me for the first time since we left his house and raised an eyebrow, questioning my statement. I smirked and stood from his car.

"I'll be at your office to finish my interview with you. Three o'clock, sharp." I spoke with my back turned to him, and before he could respond, I walked away. When I made it to my floor, my door was wide open and Anabella was moving what looked like a few old things from the place. I greeted her with a simple hello and walked straight in toward my room. I clearly couldn't talk to her about this new unexplained attraction I had for Arsen without her rude criticism. She didn't even respond when I spoke to her.

I laid back on my bed, wondering how I could possibly feel this way. This man had just threatened to take my life if I revealed his secret and I could feel nothing but lust for him after that. Was I going insane? In that brief moment of submission, I felt so alive. It was just something about the way he told me what to do and that look he gave me, like I had better listen to him or else. I wasn't sure why, but I thought I was letting my guard down. I thought I might be able to open up to someone new. Arsen was different from the rest and I thought it was time for me to actually deal with a real man.

I was definitely insane. I was risking my life, all for the sake of finding a lover who I could actually balance out with. I thought he could get over his hatred for me after seeing how trustworthy I would be with his secret. I turned on some music and started to sing along softly until I felt the presence of someone at my door.

"So you were just going to stay out all night with no call or text, then come home and not tell me where have you been?" Anabella asked from my doorway. I looked at her and shook my head.

"Ana, I called you like twenty times last night and you didn't answer the phone for me, which resulted in me staying the night at Arsen's house. I didn't think you would care to know where I've been since you ignored my phone calls and didn't even bother to respond when I just said hello to you." I rolled my eyes and continued to stare up at the ceiling.

"Did you call my new number? That would be the smart thing to do, Lola," she said. "And great. Just great. You're sleeping with this man now?"

"Since when do you have a new number and when were you going to tell me, Anabella?" I sat up quickly and looked directly at her. "I'm your best friend for Christ's sake. What if it was an emergency?! And how dare you? Nothing happened between Arsen and I!"

"I'm sure Arsen would be all the protection that you needed, Lola. And I definitely sent a text to all my contacts with my new number. You would have noticed if you had taken a break from that little novel of yours and paid attention to the real world." She scoffed. "Pathetic. I don't even know who you are anymore"

"Get out of my room, Anabella." I couldn't believe that my own best friend would even say such a thing like that to me.

She had been the only one who supported my decision to become a writer, but the last few days had been really tense between us. I wasn't sure where all of this built-up hate had come from inside of her, but I needed to find out, and I needed to know why she was directing it toward whatever Arsen and I have going on.

"Fine," she mumbled, folding her arms over her chest and leaving my bedroom.

I heard her say a few things under her breath, but I didn't care enough to extend the problem at hand. Since we were children, Anabella was always stubborn. She never cared if she was wrong or right as long as no one questioned her actions, and when her actions were questioned, she would catch an attitude. This specific problem never phased me because I was the most knowledgeable one in the friendship and she would always listen to me.

Since Arsen and I had begun talking, Anabella had taken her stubbornness to an entirely different level. She had been very moody and disapproving of everything that had been going on, although I was a grown woman who was completely capable of making her own conscious decisions. I wasn't quite sure what she didn't get about that.

Even if she didn't approve of who I was dating, she could at least support me being in a relationship—and that was the thing! Arsen and I weren't even dating, so I didn't see what the big deal was. Whatever we had between us could either go really badly or really well. All I knew was that I wished I could have my best friend there for me through it all.

I started to do a bit of studying to clear my mind, but also to gather some questions to ask Arsen. I searched his name on the internet and wrote down any interesting facts that caught my eye. I started downloading a couple of his books onto my laptop to read later. I wanted to know the ins and outs of his mind. One of his books caught my eye and I couldn't wait to read it.

The very first page caught my eye and I almost instantly fell in love with the story.

*"Idyllic is what I would describe him as." I spoke into the phone, letting out a small laugh. I was in the community kitchen of my apartment, filling up a small bucket with ice. I heard my best friend mumble, slightly confused, on the other side of the phone.*

*"You barely even know the guy, Sarah. Plus, he's like ten times your ag." She sounded irritated. I could just imagine how hard she rolled her eyes, but something drew me to this guy—my new neighbor directly across the hall. We bumped into each other once in the hallway and the way he caught me was breathtaking. I don't know what it was.*

*Guys never really caught my eye, old or young. I was always on a level that they weren't. I liked to focus on my craft more than a silly relationship, but this was something different. His rich, tan skin and glistening smile. There was a little spark when I fell into his arms. The innocence of the touch drove me up the wall and I have yet to understand why.*

*"You don't get it, Rachel. I felt something." I smiled slightly and ran a finger around the rim of the silver bucket of ice.*

*"You're irritating, you know that?" she exclaimed with a very nasty tone of voice. I rolled my eyes and took a deep breath.*

*"Look, if you're going to continue with this lurid attitude, I don't think we should finish this phone call. Bye." And with that, I hung up the phone.*

*When she made it back to her room, she opened up her journal to the entry she wrote after meeting Arthur.*

*'He was just a guy and I was just a girl.*

*No, wait, he was more than that.*

*How could I devalue a soul with rich intellect and a consciousness that glows immensely to just a gender? Something so distant, something so man-made.*

*I want to know your thoughts. I want to feel your vibrations. I want our subconscious minds to linger around each other and engage in an experience our physical bodies can't.*

*I want to talk to you. I want to hear about your childhood, I want to know your deepest conspiracies, and I want you to take up all the space in my mind.*

*Feed me knowledge. Enlighten me.'*

*Sarah smiled down at the page before she started to draw hearts all over it. She felt that Arthur was the guy of her dreams.*

The story of my life. Midway through reading, I found myself still thinking about the argument I had with Anabella again. So I decided to just let the situation go and get some rest before class and my meeting with Arsen tomorrow.

# ARSEN

Why was Lola acting so ...seductive after I practically told her that I'd kill her? Why was she so eager to see me again after she found out about my drug cartel? This was all so strange. Did she really feel this way, or was this all apart of some type of scam from my enemy? I wasn't sure what it was, but I called a meeting with the guys at the clubhouse.

I picked up a pack of beer and brought it along with me to the meeting. The guys were very anxious to hear the news that I had for them. I didn't know how they'd react or what they'd say, but I just knew I had fucked up badly. Had I not taken the time to calm down, I would've never noticed that my hand was red and burning from how tightly I was gripping the steering wheel.

I just can't believe that something like that even happened. How could I be so stupid to have practically left all of my most important information out in the open? I just thought I'd be able to trust Lola enough to not do anything stupid like that, but boy was my judgment wrong. I started to think about how my entire empire could come crashing down if the world found out about this, and I became so angry that I just had to hurry inside before I lost my temper.

In the clubhouse, the guys and I gathered around the table. They all took seats while I stood before them. I put my hands behind my back and cleared my throat. I was afraid to tell them the news, but I knew that I had to be strong in front of them. My team would never do anything to me. I just had never told them news like this before so it was a new experience for me. This could also spark a new emotion that I had never seen in them.

How easy could it really be to break news like this to them? How could I tell them our future lives were in danger?

"All right, guys, here's the bad news." They all sighed and threw up their arms in anger. "I know. Bad news is a rare thing around here, but we are in serious trouble now."

"What kind of trouble, boss?" Pete, one of the members, asked.

"So, there's this girl who I met after doing a seminar at her school a couple of days ago and she's gorgeous. I mean, the most beautiful girl I have ever laid eyes on." I took a deep breath and continued. "To make a long story short, we went on a date and she came home with me. I let her stay in my home while I was at work today."

"Well why would you do that, boss?" David, another member, said.

"Don't ask. Anyway, I caught her going through my email and she found out about this drug cartel." I shook my head and took a deep breath waiting for their response.

All of the men gasped and looked around at each other. I could see the anger in their faces, but also the worry. A couple of men started discussing with each other what could go wrong if anyone else found out, and it felt like the weight of the world came crashing down on my shoulders. I knew that I had really messed up.

"What are we going to do about this? What are we going to do to the girl? No one can find out about this." Pete sounded confused, looking around at all of us.

"I say we kill the girl. If she isn't that popular around the school or if she's a nobody in general, there should be no problem if she dies. Right?" one of the other members spoke. The group waited in silence for my response

"Kill her?! I think we've killed enough people already," I said, covering the fact that I wanted to save her life because of the feelings I had towards her. "Plus, there's something really special about this girl."

"You like her or something?" Pete asked.

"That's beside the point here, Pete."

"I say you kidnap the girl. There's like a week left in school, right? Kidnap the girl and no one at the school will come looking for her because it's the summertime," David spoke up. "There's no point in killing the girl when you can use her to work for you"

I ran my index finger and thumb over my chin. "Hmm, sounds like a pretty cool idea."

All of the guys simultaneously agreed that that would be the best option and we began to plan it out. The guys and I came up with the best way possible to get Lola to fall for this trap. Tomorrow at our interview I would see if Lola would come over to my place for dinner after her last day of classes. Then I would explain to her that she was going to stay and work for me until everything was settled between us. Hopefully, some other things would happen between us, but I'd save that for later.

**If you want to continue reading this story, you can get your copy from your favorite vendor by searching for the title:**

A Billionaire's Treasure
An Alpha Billionaire Romance

You can also find the e-book version by typing this link in your computer's browser:
https://www.hotandsteamyromance.com/products/a-billionaire-s-treasure-an-alpha-billionaire-romance

# OTHER BOOKS BY THIS AUTHOR

### Saving Her Rescuer: A Billionaire & A Virgin Romance

I was just trying to get away from my crazy ex for the weekend when I ended up in a giant pileup on the highway up to Gore Mountain.

https://geni.us/SavingHerRescuer

~

### Sensual Sounds: A Rockstar Ménage

Lust. Lies. Double lives.

The rock and roll industry is full of people who are looking out for themselves and willing to do anything to rise to the top.

https://www.hotandsteamyromance.com/collections/frontpage/products/sensual-sounds-a-rockstar-menage

~

### On the Run: A Secret Baby Romance

Murder. Lies. Fraud. Just another day in the lives of billionaires and women on the run.

https://www.hotandsteamyromance.com/collections/frontpage/products/on-the-run-a-secret-baby-romance

The Dirty Doctor's Touch: A Billionaire Doctor Romance

I am a master. An elitist. I am at the top of my field, and I know what I am doing.

https://www.hotandsteamyromance.com/collections/frontpage/products/the-dirty-doctor-s-touch-a-billionaire-doctor-romance

The Hero She Needs: A Single Daddy Next Door Romance

He's the only man I've ever wanted…

https://www.hotandsteamyromance.com/collections/frontpage/products/the-hero-she-needs-a-single-daddy-next-door-romance

You can find all of my books here:

Hot and Steamy Romance

https://www.hotandsteamyromance.com

Facebook

facebook.com/HotAndSteamyRomance

# COPYRIGHT

©Copyright 2020 by Celeste Fall - All rights Reserved

In no way is it legal to reproduce, duplicate, or transmit any part of this document in either electronic means or in printed format. Recording of this publication is strictly prohibited and any storage of this document is not allowed unless with written permission from the publisher. All rights are reserved. Respective authors own all copyrights not held by the publisher.

www.ingramcontent.com/pod-product-compliance
Lightning Source LLC
LaVergne TN
LVHW011716060526
838200LV00051B/2921